While Nellie Starr and her family are fictitious, their journey on the Cherokee Trail of Tears reflects the experiences of many Cherokee who were relocated from their homes in the southeastern United States to Indian Territory in present-day Oklahoma.

After the Indian Removal Act of 1830 was signed by President Andrew Jackson, the Cherokee appealed to the courts to keep their homelands. But the 1835 Treaty of New Echota, which was signed by a minority group of the Cherokee but called a false treaty by the majority, sealed the fate of the Cherokee. They were ordered to leave their homes. Soldiers rounded up the Cherokee, took them to holding camps, and then started groups on their way west.

Three groups were escorted by the military. Principal Chief John Ross negotiated for the Cherokee to be in charge of the rest of the treks westward. One of the leaders was Reverend Jesse Bushyhead. From the autumn of 1838 into the harsh winter of 1839, thirteen groups of about one thousand members each traveled to their new land set aside by Congress to separate the Indians from white settlers.

SISTERS IN TIME

Nellie
the Brave
THE CHEROKEE TRAIL OF TEARS

VEDA BOYD JONES

BARBOUR
PUBLISHING

Nellie
the Brave

To my W&W friends: Vicki Grove and Cheryl Harness

Cover design by Lookout Design Group, Inc.

Published by Barbour Publishing, Inc., P.O. Box 719, Uhrichsville, Ohio 44683
www.barbourbooks.com

Our mission is to publish and distribute inspirational products offering exceptional value and biblical encouragement to the masses.

Member of the
Evangelical Christian
Publishers Association

Printed in the United States of America.
5 4 3 2 1

CONTENTS

CHAPTER 1
The Roundup

Tennessee 1838

"They're here!" Nellie Starr whispered. She peeked around the curtain of her upstairs bedroom window at the soldiers. She counted five men, all on horseback, riding purposefully up the lane toward the house. "They've come for us."

"Will they hurt us?" Sarah asked.

"Yes. No! They won't hurt us physically," Nellie assured her five-year-old sister. "But they will change everything. Everything! Hurry. Keep packing."

"Can I take my doll?"

"Yes, but hurry. Put those clothes in here." She motioned to the black horsehair trunk where she had placed her day dresses and her Sunday dress of blue muslin. She added her papers and pen. She couldn't endure the long trip without writing. And she'd write in Cherokee language, using Sequoyah's syllabary, not English, so the soldiers wouldn't know what she was writing.

A loud knock, more like pounding, sounded a moment before the front door was opened with great force. The door swung so wide it hit the wall beside it with a big bang.

"Nellie!" Etsi, her mother, yelled. Nellie fairly flew down the stairs to the front room. Etsi faced three soldiers. Two stood on the porch.

"It's time to go," one soldier said. "Where's your man to hitch up the wagon?"

Etsi looked at Nellie.

"He wants to know where Edoda is." Nellie translated the soldier's words into her native Cherokee language. Her mother understood some English, but Etsi's command of the language didn't match Nellie's. Nellie had studied hard at the mission school and spoke the best English of all the students, even better than those older than her twelve years. Her teacher said she had a gift for language, and Nellie cherished the gift that let her speak easily with the missionaries.

"Father's in the smokehouse," Nellie told the soldiers. "I'll go get him."

"Mason!" a soldier yelled to a man on the porch. "Get the man in the smokehouse!" He turned back to Nellie. "Let's get going."

"But we're not yet packed."

"You're as packed as you're going to be," another soldier said.

Nellie ignored the man's words and addressed the soldier who had spoken first. More brass on his uniform told her he was in charge.

"Please give us the rest of the day to get ready."

He shook his head, and the second soldier laughed. "As if they haven't had all the time in the world already, Lieutenant Seward."

"One hour," Lieutenant Seward said.

"One hour," Nellie translated to Etsi.

"That's not long enough," Nellie said.

"You've had two years, a month, some days, and now one hour," the lieutenant said.

That was true, but it wasn't true. The false treaty signed by only a few Cherokee—not the rightful leaders—gave them two years to move to Indian Territory west of the Mississippi River. But during those two years, thousands of Cherokee had signed a petition to Congress, saying the treaty to sell their lands to the white men was not a real treaty. The Cherokee had hoped that they would not be forced off the land of their forefathers. Now, there was no more hope.

One hour to pack up a lifetime of memories. Nellie glanced at the clock on the fireplace mantle in the front room. Just after nine o'clock. Before noon, they would be on their way to a new land.

Nellie heard a whimper and saw Sarah on the stair landing, her face crumpled, tears of fear dripping from her chin onto her dress.

"It will be fine, Sarah. Go pack." Sarah climbed the few steps to the top. "Hurry," Nellie said.

"We must pack more dishes," Etsi said and turned, her sweeping skirts making a swishing sound as she walked away.

Nellie told the soldiers they were going to the kitchen, and the men followed them to the back of the house.

The kitchen was already stifling in the unseasonably hot June morning. Spring had come early to the hills, and crops had been put in early without any bud getting nipped by a late frost. Summer had come just as early, and the heat of the house was nearly unbearable. Nellie wiped sweat from her forehead with her hand.

Etsi had been putting dishes in a wooden box. She continued packing, wrapping dishes in old newspapers they had saved because they were in the Cherokee language. That way they would have reading material in the new land.

The soldiers sat in ladder-back chairs around the oblong wooden table. Earlier, Nellie had drawn water in the well bucket, and now she poured glasses of cool water for the men. She hoped her hospitality would gain them more time.

One of the men who worked at Edoda's general store had stormed from town not long after breakfast. He had shouted from his horse that the soldiers were rounding up Cherokee, and then he had galloped to his home.

They had immediately set to work. Edoda had run to the field to drive the oxen toward the barn where their wagon sat in readiness for such a sad day as this. Then he ran to the smokehouse to gather food.

From the kitchen window, Nellie saw a soldier point his rifle at Edoda as he followed Edoda out of the tool shed. They headed toward the barn.

"Candle molds. We'll need those," Etsi said. "And let's throw in the candles already made. And the butter churn, but it won't fit in the box. And those pots."

Nellie went around the room, handing items to Etsi, who shifted things to make room in the box for more. The cast-iron pots were too heavy to pack in a box, and Nellie carried them to the front porch, then returned.

"What about the stove?" Nellie stood by the cast-iron cookstove. How could they load the boxes and trunks and still have room for the stove? And how would they cook if they didn't have it?

"I don't know. We'll ask Edoda when he comes in." Etsi put a bag of healing herbs in the brown wooden box and then walked to the front room.

14

Nellie scurried after her. A quick glance told her there was no way they could load the furniture on the wagon. Too much, too big. They'd need five wagons to fit everything, and that wouldn't do it, either. They could take only the wooden crate Edoda had carried in before the soldiers came. Now to decide what to pack in the crate.

Tick-tock, tick-tock. She reached for the mantle clock. It quit ticking when she tilted it, the pendulum stopping its measured swing. The clock needed winding every eight days. If only she could stop time like she had stopped this clock. If only she could turn back time to the last day Edoda had wound the clock. Then there would be no Cherokee removal demanded by the United States government.

But she couldn't stop time. And now she didn't know how much of the hour was left for packing. She carefully took the weight out of the back of the clock and wrapped it in her handkerchief. She put the clock and the separate weight in the packing crate.

Etsi stood by the stuffed chair where Edoda liked to sit in the evenings. She ran her fingers lovingly across the back and looked at the room slowly, her gaze moving inch by inch as if memorizing every chair and stool and table and picture.

"Etsi, we have to hurry. Hurry."

"We should take the sampler you embroidered," she said and slowly took the framed fabric off the wall and placed it in the crate. "Is your room finished?"

"I'll check on Sarah's stuff. What about Lewis's room?"

"Lewis!" Etsi exclaimed and put her hand to her mouth, covering a moan.

He had left for Old Rivers's house before the warning had

come. He'd gone to take the old man an herbal potion that Etsi had mixed for his cold.

"He'll be back any minute. He's been gone long enough." But that was if he didn't dawdle along the way with the other boys in the area if they happened to be down by the creek, which would surely be the way he came home. And there were always other boys around Lewis.

Tears pooled in Etsi's eyes, and Nellie hugged her, then said, "I'll pack his clothes."

She passed a soldier, who had come into the front room to investigate the packing, and climbed the stairs two at a time. She found Sarah in the bedroom they shared, crying in a corner.

"We don't have time for that," Nellie said. She held her little sister for a long moment. "I need your help packing Lewis's clothes."

Sarah sniffed and wiped her cheeks with the back of her hands but followed Nellie to Lewis's room across the hall. "Where's Lewis?"

"He'll be back. We'll use the satchel for his things."

They tossed shirts and trousers into the bag. "There's no room for his coat. He'll have to get a new one when we get to the territory." The thought of replacing the old things gave Nellie new courage. "Hurry."

She heard the rumble of the oxen and the creaking of the white canvas-covered wagon and looked out Lewis's window at Edoda driving the team out of the barn toward the house. The wagon had been packed with things they weren't using day to day but would need later. Now they'd have to load the boxes and trunks they had packed this morning.

"We can carry our trunk down," Nellie said. But it was heavier than she'd imagined. Sarah struggled to carry one end, so they scooted more than carried the trunk to the stairs, where it thumped down to the first floor. They pushed it out the door and left it on the porch. Nellie ran back upstairs to get Lewis's satchel.

What about the bedding? Where would they sleep? They didn't need covers now with the June sun heating the earth, but what about next winter in their new home? Nellie gazed at Lewis's bed and pulled off the blanket. Hadn't the teachers at the mission said that the government would give them blankets and food for the trip and supplies when they reached the new land?

But it would be good to have their own blankets, and they could easily be thrown over the boxes in the wagon. They wouldn't take up much extra room. She grabbed Lewis's coat, too.

She took the blankets from the other beds. In her room, she grabbed the blanket but paused a brief moment to look out the window.

Memorize the trees, memorize the lane, memorize the robin that built a nest outside your window, her heart told her. *You will never see them again.* Her head told her to carry the blankets to the porch. She ran downstairs, arms full, and piled the blankets outside on the trunk, then found Etsi and Sarah in the parlor, doing nothing, just standing there, holding each other. Nothing more was in the crate. A soldier sat in Edoda's chair.

"Etsi, are your clothes ready to go?" Nellie asked.

"I don't think so."

"Let's get them packed." She took her etsi's arm and led her to the stairs.

"Nellie," Edoda called from the kitchen.

Nellie gave Etsi a nudge to urge her up the stairs. "Help her, Sarah," she said and scurried to the kitchen.

"Could you help me with these heavy boxes?" Edoda asked, an urgency in his voice.

Two soldiers still sat at the kitchen table, but neither offered to help. Their expressions showed impatience, and Nellie sensed that if her family didn't get their things loaded soon, they would be forced to leave boxes behind.

"We don't carry," one of the soldiers said. "Orders." As if that explained not helping a girl and her edoda pack a wagon.

The solid wooden box of dishes and silverware and other kitchen things was heavy. Even with Edoda's strength, it took both of them to wield it out the door. The height of the back porch was nearly the same as the wagon, so they had to lift the box only a few inches, which was a good thing. Nellie didn't know how they could have lifted it any higher.

One soldier stood at the head of the matched set of reddish-colored oxen, holding them still. Lieutenant Seward walked out on the porch, his boots making a heavy clunking noise.

"Mason, you and Willis go to the next farm and get them moving. We can't take all day getting this section to the camp."

The soldier holding the oxen left with another man, and Nellie climbed onto the wagon to hold the reins. Edoda loaded another box on his own and moved some tools around to find a small place for the churn.

"There's a trunk out front," Nellie said. "And pots."

"First I want a few more tools," Edoda said. He ran to the tool shed, his black hat with the crow feather bobbing up and down with every fast step. He returned carrying a hoe and a hatchet.

"No hatchet," Lieutenant Seward said and pointed at the porch. "No weapons allowed."

Nellie translated for her father so there was no misunderstanding, although he knew a fair amount of English and probably understood just fine. If he couldn't take the ax, he surely couldn't take his gun to hunt game, and she didn't want a confrontation about it.

"How do we clear land for a new house without tools?" Edoda asked softly in Cherokee, so softly he may not have intended the soldier to hear, but Nellie repeated his question in English.

"There will be supplies in Indian Territory. You don't have to take everything. The government will pay you for what's left."

Edoda took a couple steps toward the shed.

"Leave it here." The lieutenant pointed at the porch again.

"It would be safer in the shed," Nellie said.

"It won't matter," Lieutenant Seward said. "Scavengers will take it."

A wave of resentment washed over Nellie, followed by a wave of intense sadness.

"Drive around front, Nellie," Edoda said, his voice hard. "Hurry."

"Hee-ah!" Nellie shouted at the team, and they strained against the yoke. She did not often drive the wagon, but Edoda said that everyone must know how to handle stock, so he had taught her the commands for the animals and the way to jerk on the reins or pull them tight.

Nellie pulled the wagon next to the front porch and tied the team to the front rail. She jumped off and ran inside, up the stairs, where Etsi and Sarah were tossing clothes into another trunk.

"Hurry," she said. "What else goes from here?"

Etsi turned dark, soulful eyes to her. "Is Lewis back?"

19

"Not yet. Any minute, though. Let's get this downstairs."

They pushed, pulled, and tugged the big trunk to the stairs, where it thumped from step to step as they guided it down.

Edoda loaded it onto the wagon and then came into the parlor, where Nellie was looking around for what other small items they could take in the packing crate.

"There's no more room," Edoda said. "We'll have to leave that crate here."

"We must take the clock," Nellie said and fished it out of the crate, along with the clock weight. On a shelf, she spied the glass bottle with the silver inlay that Edoda had brought back when he went to Washington to meet with the government people. She was unsure what it had held at one time but thought it was probably perfume. It had been empty since she could remember, but the lacy silver on the glass had fascinated her, and she had played with it many times, twirling it to see the lovely patterns. She carefully wrapped it and the clock and the weight in a blanket and stuffed them in a corner of the wagon.

"What about the crops?" Edoda asked.

Even though there had been no rain lately, the corn was knee-high due to the early spring. They had already picked two varieties of beans, and the squash and cucumber vines had flowered and now reached across the rows.

Nellie asked the lieutenant about the beans.

"Leave the crops for the next family," he said, looking Nellie straight in the eyes, then shaking his head and looking down at the ground. "We've got to go."

"My brother isn't back from our neighbor's house," Nellie said.

"We can't wait. He may already be rounded up and sent along. You'll catch up to him, or he'll catch up to you."

"Surely we can wait a few more minutes," Nellie said, but the soldier ignored her and climbed on his horse, motioning for the other men to mount their own horses.

"We'll pass him on the road," Nellie assured her mother, whose tears flowed silently down her angular cheeks.

Etsi helped Sarah climb to the seat of the covered wagon, and then she climbed up.

"The lamps," Edoda said and went back into the house.

Of course, they would need lamps. They weren't thinking. None of them were thinking of all the things they would need in the new place. Buckets. They'd need the well bucket.

Nellie ran to the kitchen and got the bucket and ladle, spilling water in the front room as she hurried back to the wagon. Edoda was tying the kerosene lamps to the side of the wagon. He tied the bucket on the other side, then climbed on board. Nellie untied the team and tossed the reins to Edoda.

"I didn't lock the door," Edoda said.

"It won't matter," Lieutenant Seward said and shook his head. "Someone would just break it down."

Nellie declined when Edoda offered her a hand to climb on the wagon. "I'll walk a ways," she said. The team already had a heavy burden to haul. No use adding to it.

They formed an odd parade. Lieutenant Seward led the way with another soldier riding beside him. Then came the wagon, followed by Nellie. A mounted soldier brought up the rear. He led two ponies, which belonged to Nellie and Sarah. Nellie felt she should be riding her pony, Midnight, but a new stubbornness inside her—or was it fear?—wouldn't let her ask the soldier for the right to ride her own pony.

Where was Edoda's horse? Probably in the far pasture and not by the barn. How could Edoda bear to leave his horse? But a glance at Edoda's hard face made her decide he was thinking of much more than his horse.

Every few steps, Nellie looked over her shoulder. Was this the last she would see of the house that Edoda had built with such pride? They had lived in the old log cabin while Edoda had worked on this house. It was modeled after the houses he had seen on his trip East, where white people lived. Now would other people move into their fine house, sleep in their beds? Cook in their kitchen? Why was this happening to them? These were the lands of their forefathers. Why were the whites driving them out at gunpoint?

Nellie picked up a small white stone from the lane, then another and another. She tucked five stones into her dress pocket. One for every member of the family. This was a part of her home-land she would take with her.

As she looked ahead, she heard a moan, a moan from her mother that rose in pitch and strength and echoed in Nellie's heart.

"Lewis!" Etsi cried. "Lewis!" Fresh tears of grief flowed down Etsi's cheeks. Sarah was gripping her doll, her shoulders shaking with sobs. Edoda turned for a look back, and Nellie saw a silent tear snake down his cheek. She put a hand to her face and swiped at her own tears.

CHAPTER 2
The First Step

Nellie's family was not yet out of their own lane when they met three white men with two wagons. Lieutenant Seward did not give an inch but made the white scavengers take to the side and drive their wagons into the pasture.

Nellie was glad they were around the big curve of the lane so she couldn't see the men go into the house. Would they take her four-poster bed? Would they take Edoda's special chair? Hatred gripped her heart, and it was not a good feeling. She clamped her jaw, her teeth grinding together.

What had happened to her in the last hour? She was a Christian girl who valued peace in her heart and pleasant thoughts for others. But she didn't feel like that girl anymore. She tried to smile to change her thoughts, but her mouth felt fixed in a frown.

They came to the main road, and she was stunned to see other Cherokee and soldier parades as odd as their own marching by. No, not marching—stumbling, shuffling, hobbling along. Old women were crying and carrying bundles on their backs. Young children who weren't on wagons walked alongside their mothers without a sound, as if they knew the importance of saying a final good-bye to their homeland.

She knew these people. They were neighbors, but no one stopped to talk. No one waved a friendly hand.

Lieutenant Seward dashed off to talk with the lead soldier,

leaving them to watch the procession. At least seven different households passed by, stirring up the dust of the road behind them, before Lieutenant Seward motioned to Edoda to fall in line.

"Hee-ah!" Edoda yelled to the oxen, turning them onto the main road.

Nellie would have waited for the dust to settle, but the soldier behind her told her to get moving. She walked on the side, away from the slight June breeze that carried the dust to the north.

Lieutenant Seward yelled back that he was going on to another farm, and he left only the soldier with the ponies to guard them. For just an instant, Nellie thought of running to the woods behind the house and hiding. Back to her old life and away from what she sensed was going to be a hard time full of problems. But that would mean deserting her family, and right now the problem that made a sob catch in her throat was Lewis. Where was he?

Would he take the road back from Old Rivers's place or ride his pony through the woods on the animal path down by the creek? She should have left a note for him, but would he even go in the house if he saw men stealing their furniture? Would he try something foolish, as he was known to do—act without thinking of the consequences? Demand that the men put their things back? What would happen then? She tried to turn her mind from bad thoughts to good ones, but that was hard to do. After all, it was her fault that Lewis wasn't with them.

She should have taken the medicine potion to Old Rivers, but she had wanted to work on her poem, and she had asked Lewis to take it to the old man who lived two farms away. Besides, there was a special tie between Old Rivers and Lewis. She had seen it before in the silent way they seemed to communicate. And Lewis had jumped at the chance to go see the old Cherokee. But where was he now?

At the next farm lane, another wagon joined them, and Nellie hung back to talk with John Deerborn, who was a boy her age and in her class at school. They had been friends for as long as she could remember. She would be of marriageable age soon, and in the privacy of her fanciful thoughts, she had wondered if John would be her future husband.

He was astride a pony, but he jumped down and walked alongside her, leading his pony by the reins. The soldiers who ordered the Deerborns to fall in line rode quickly to the front to talk with the soldier in charge.

Nellie explained about Lewis, but John had not seen him.

"We had no time to grab many things," John complained. "They just appeared and said to come now."

"Were you already packed?" Nellie asked, nodding at the wagon.

"We had an hour, they said, but we were rushed out before the time was up. Oh," he wailed, "I forgot Grandfather's feathers!"

"The eagle feathers?" She had heard John speak of the special collection that his grandfather had given him before he died. They had ceremonial medicine, his grandfather had told him. Nellie didn't believe that for a moment, but she knew John did.

His wail grew louder. "We will have hard times."

"You can get more feathers," Nellie said. "The land we're going to must have many eagles."

"Are there fine mountains like these?" he asked and pointed at the ridge to the east in the forest highlands. "Eagles must have high mountains for their nests."

"We will find some along the way," Nellie said. "I'll help you climb to their aerie."

"But Grandfather's feathers had special powers," John said.

"Remember what the mission teachers said? Only God has special powers."

John hung his head. "I believe that, but I also believe there is something in the feathers. Can I not believe both?"

It didn't seem reasonable to Nellie that both could be true, but how could she disagree with a boy whose face was streaked with dust and tears?

"The feathers only have the powers that God puts in them," she said. "I think He gave the eagles such a powerful wing spread so they could soar high. And He gave the feathers special meaning to you so you could soar, too. They are a symbol, like the Christian cross is a symbol." She felt good about her explanation. And she thought the teachers at the mission would approve.

"That sounds right," he said. "And God knows where Lewis is and will bring him this way."

"Yes," Nellie agreed, but it was easier to think about the feathers than it was to think that Lewis was on his way to join them.

They walked on and on. Another wagon joined them. Old Rivers's son drove it, and Old Rivers sat beside him, even though the old man looked tired and sick from his cold. He bent over with a hoarse cough. Nothing worse than a cold in the summer, Etsi often said. But where was Lewis? There was no sign of Lewis or his horse.

Nellie hung back and shouted, "Where is Lewis?"

"He went home," Old Rivers said, "right before the soldiers came."

Nellie shook her head to say he had not arrived. Had he seen the soldiers and hung out in the woods?

The line of wagons grew longer, and as they passed through an area where the poorer Cherokee lived, the number of walkers grew. Some families had only what they could carry. How would they start over with nothing?

Some of the Cherokee men wore red turbans. Others wore blue, and still others wore nothing atop their coal black hair. Some were dressed like the whites, but many wore traditional deerskin leggings and embroidered hunting shirts. The women wore long skirts that dragged in the dirt as their postures slumped and their sad heads hung low from their shoulders. The sounds of moans and sobbing rose over the clanking of the chains on the wagons, the creaking of the wheels, the neighing of the horses, the grunts of the oxen, and the shouted orders of the soldiers to keep moving.

Nellie's stomach growled. The sun was high overhead, past straight up. It had already started its way toward the west. The soldiers did not pause for something to eat. Only once did they halt the group by a spring so they could get water.

Nellie joined her family, and they drank all they could, then filled the gray water bucket to the brim. As the wagon lurched along, water splashed over the sides of the bucket until it reached a level where it sloshed back and forth but didn't leave a wet trail.

The dust grew thicker as their wagon train caught up to the one ahead, and the shuffling feet of the people and the animals stirred up the ground. Nellie watched her step as the animals left their droppings on the road.

She had drunk so much water, she had to relieve herself. At first it was just a normal full feeling inside her, but as she walked and walked, the feeling intensified until she could hardly put one foot in front of the other. She could go behind a tree in the woods beside the road, but would the soldier shoot her if she left the group?

Shouting out the question to the soldier with the ponies was the only way to solve this problem. She was glad that John had fallen back with some other boys and wouldn't see her humiliation.

She made her way to the soldier and spoke in English, hoping the Cherokee around her wouldn't have a clear understanding of her words.

The soldier smirked but motioned her to go to the woods. Without waiting to tell Etsi, she made a break for the woods. She didn't stop at the first trees but went deep inside the woods for privacy, and still she was uneasy that someone would see her.

What a relief! When she made her way back to the road, the soldier with the ponies had fallen toward the back and was waiting for her to rejoin the marchers.

She hurried, half-walking and half-running, to her place next to their wagon. Sarah was squirming on the seat by Etsi, who still shed big tears of fear and sadness. Walking as close to the wagon as she dared, Nellie called to her mother. "I can take Sarah to the woods if she needs to go!"

Etsi nodded, and Edoda slowed the team. Sarah jumped into Nellie's arms, and the two girls walked into the woods.

Nellie stood lookout for Sarah and listened to the caws of two crows crying out to each other. Were they sharing the news that the Cherokee were leaving their beloved homes? When the girls emerged from the woods, Nellie could see the line of wagons and her people stretching all the way back to the big curve in the road.

"Hurry," she told her sister. "We don't want to be away from Etsi and Edoda. We might lose them in all these people."

"Is. . .Lewis. . .lost?" Sarah asked breathlessly as they ran to catch up with the Starr wagon.

"God. . .will bring him. . .to us. Just give him. . .some time. He will. . .catch up. . .with us."

The girls slowed to a walk to catch their breath.

"Lewis is on his pony," Sarah said. "Blaze can run as fast as the wind. Etsi is so sad for Lewis."

"I know, but there is nothing we can do. We must pray for Lewis to join us and pray that this trip does not take too long. Are you hungry?"

"Etsi gave me some cornbread. There's more. You want to ride now? Walking is too hard. Too hard to keep up with the wagon."

They walked faster. When they reached the Starr wagon, Edoda slowed down, and Nellie helped her sister aboard. Sarah said something to Etsi that Nellie couldn't hear. Then Etsi reached into a satchel and handed a square of cornbread to Nellie.

She ate greedily as she walked along. It tasted wonderful—not as good as fresh-made cornbread, but even better because she was hungry. With that need satisfied, her thoughts turned once more to Lewis. Where was he?

He was a good boy, really. Nellie squabbled with him some, but that was just because he was a boy. He had privileges that she was not allowed, and he was a year younger. He could run in the fields, go on overnight hunting trips, and ride his pony to Edoda's general store most anytime. She was stuck in the house, which was where she liked to be most of the time, but not doing chores like cooking and sewing. She liked her books and her writing materials. And she couldn't think of a place she'd rather be than in her room at the writing desk Edoda had made for her.

But Lewis? He didn't like to read much, even though he could read Cherokee. He hadn't taken to the mission school the way Nellie had, hanging on to every word of the teachers, and he hadn't taken to English like she had. He liked playing stickball, which got brutal with the boys hustling for the ball and sometimes resulted in broken bones. And he liked hunting with his blowgun. He also liked riding Blaze. His pony had a flame-like white streak on its long face, which is why Lewis picked the name. Lewis was the best rider in the family, even better than Edoda, really.

Oh, no. She hadn't packed his blowgun. Well, he'd just have to make another when they arrived at the new land. The white men who had headed for their house probably took it. And they had probably taken Nellie's writing desk for some white girl to use. A huge sob shook Nellie's shoulders at the thought that she would never again sit at her desk and write a poem.

The mission teachers had read some poetry of Phillis Wheatley, and although most of it had to do with someone dealing with death, the poems had touched Nellie. She had written some of her own and had named them like Phillis had named hers: "To Edoda on the Death of Old Roany, Our Cow," "On Imagination," "On the Day of the First Corn." She had been working on that last one when the store worker arrived and told them the soldiers were coming. Now Lewis was gone, and the house was gone, and their life as they knew it was gone. What would happen to them?

Nellie's thoughts tumbled along as she put one heavy foot in front of the other. She was tired, and the sun was moving down the western sky. Where would they make camp for the night?

Where were they going? And where was Lewis?

How far had she walked? Much farther than to the mission school, which was around three miles. That walk took about an hour, and they had been on the move for much longer than that. She thought they had covered at least twelve miles, and if her estimate was right, by the time the lead soldier finally called a halt for the night, they had covered around fifteen miles.

CHAPTER 3
The First Camp

"We're less than six or seven miles to the Hiwassee," one soldier said. He and another soldier had ridden close to Nellie.

"But it will be dark in a few minutes," the second soldier said. "This camp is as good as the one by the river. The spring is good."

Nellie thought that soldier must have some Cherokee in him. He recognized the time of silence—sunset—when the wind lay down and day creatures settled in their nests and night creatures stirred before venturing out. It was the time when people needed a deep rest.

In the twilight, Edoda followed the other wagons onto pasture land beside the dirt road. He unhitched the oxen and staked them not far from the wagon. This was the first rest the poor animals had had all day.

In all, Nellie thought there were maybe two hundred Cherokee in the camp, but there were only some twenty wagons. Many who had joined their caravan during the long afternoon were on foot without their belongings. How would they start over without some keepsakes from their homes?

She knew the government had promised supplies for a year in the new territory, but she was glad her family had packed the fine dishes that Etsi cherished, to add a touch of home in the new house. Looking around at some of the other Cherokee, she felt guilty for even thinking of the glass dishes.

There were some mighty poor Cherokee on this wagon train. Some of the children were thin, too thin, and their clothing was dirty. She looked down at her gingham dress and saw that it was also dirty from the dusty road.

Soldiers carrying flaming torches escorted those Cherokee who were fortunate enough to have water buckets. *The clear spring is marvelous,* Nellie thought, when it was her turn to walk down in the shallow valley to fill the water bucket. She splashed cool water on her face. Never had water felt so good. It revived her sagging spirit.

Nellie carried the full bucket to the top of the hill and shared the water with the Cherokee around the campfire Edoda had built. Then she went back down the hill to refill the bucket.

Etsi poured part of the second bucket in one of the pots she dug out of the wagon and put it on the fire. Edoda secretively whittled chunks of meat off a shoulder ham that he had rescued from the smokehouse, hiding his knife the moment he had enough ham for the soup. Nellie wondered how he had slipped it by the soldiers.

Etsi added the meat to the water. While it cooked, she went from group to group, looking for Lewis. No one had seen him. She returned to the campfire with tears in her eyes.

"Old Rivers," Etsi said to the aged Cherokee who sat next to the fire, "when did he leave your cabin?" She had asked him that as soon as the wagons had stopped and she could make her way to his side. Now she asked it again.

"He gave me the potion and left," Old Rivers explained once again with a shake of his head. He coughed before he was able to continue. "He is out there, waiting, watching." He raised a gnarly finger and pointed away from the road.

"Watching for what?" Sarah asked.

Old Rivers shrugged his shoulders and glanced at the soldier who stood nearby. His eyes glinted in the firelight, and the dancing flames made his lined face seem not so lined, but the cough continued.

"Should I get the bowls and spoons?" Nellie asked. "Which box are they in?"

"Under too many things," Etsi said. "We'll drink the soup."

Edoda dug out three metal cups from under the wagon seat. Etsi asked a prayer of blessing over the food, and the Cherokee sitting around their campfire took turns drinking their supper.

"Is there cornbread?" Sarah asked.

"We'll save what little there is for morning," Etsi said. With the soup gone, she put more water in the pot. When it was hot, she added herbs to make a healing drink for Old Rivers.

Although the June night was warm, Nellie was glad she'd grabbed the blankets to make a soft bed on the grass. She climbed in the wagon and handed them down to Etsi. Carefully, she unwrapped the clock and silver-laced glass bottle. She put the prized possessions under the wagon seat to rewrap the next morning.

For a long time, Nellie lay on the pallet beside Sarah, staring at the fire. When the last ember died, she stared at the sky and the bright stars that twinkled overhead. She had never slept outdoors before. Before the big house, home was the old cabin. There had never been a reason not to sleep in a bed.

Now the night sounds seemed louder than ever before, even though she had slept many a summer night with the window as wide as it would open to let in the night breezes. She liked hearing the chirping crickets and the lonely *whoo* of the owl in the woods behind their house. But now, the sounds were close and seemed threatening without the protection of a roof and a floor.

She knew many of the Cherokee around them had kept the old ways, traveling some and camping away from their cabins, but her family had stayed at home. Edoda rode to town each afternoon to check with the men who worked in his general store and to do accounts, but he preferred country living to town living, so they had always lived away from town.

Old Rivers had taken Lewis on overnight hunting trips. Edoda had said that a Cherokee boy must learn the ways of the hunter, but he seemed glad that Old Rivers had been the one to teach Lewis. That was really the Cherokee way. Male relatives of young boys taught them fishing and hunting and fighting. Edoda hunted with a gun, while many Cherokee, including Old Rivers, were experts with a bow and arrow.

Lewis knew the stars that were twinkling down on Nellie. He called groupings by names that Old Rivers had taught him. One evening, he had shown the Bear to Nellie, but she had a hard time seeing a bear in the sky. She was much better with words. She could read something about a bear and be taken to a forest in her mind, seeing the bear stand on its back legs, reaching for honey in a tree—or with its cubs.

She hoped there was no bear around here. Bears didn't come around big groups of people, did they? She dreamed of bears when she finally fell asleep. She dreamed of Lewis chasing a bear up a tree.

At first morning light, the camp came to life. Edoda carried water from the spring and gathered firewood.

"No time for fires today!" a soldier yelled, and another echoed the command around the camp. "Load up!"

The soldiers chewed on beef jerky, but the Cherokee ate only what they had with them. Etsi passed out the last of the cornbread to the family and to Old Rivers and his son.

"What will we eat later?" Sarah asked.

"We'll make a fire again tonight," Edoda said, "and cook more stew."

Old Rivers coughed, and oddly enough, it didn't seem as harsh as it had the day before.

"You make more medicine tonight," he said to Etsi.

"Yes. We'll have a fire then."

Nellie held the oxen while Edoda put the yoke on them. This was a job for Lewis or one of the hired men, not for her. Edoda had three Cherokee hired to work the fields. Other men that Edoda did business with had black African slaves for that type of labor, but Edoda said it was not Christian, even though there were slaves in the Bible. He said it was no more fitting that someone dominate a black person than it was for a white person to dominate the red-skinned Cherokee.

Their hired men had hurried to their homes the moment the store worker had shouted that the soldiers were coming. So here her family was, with no one to help with the oxen except her. That made Lewis's absence echo in Nellie's mind, and she ground her teeth in anger for what was happening to them. Where was Lewis?

With the oxen in place, Nellie helped load the blankets and once again wrapped the clock and the bottle so they wouldn't break.

A soldier shouted for the Cherokee to fall into line on the road. Nellie waited beside the Starr wagon until Edoda's turn to urge the oxen into the road. Right behind them this time was Old Rivers and his son.

The morning started out the same as yesterday's forced march had ended. Clouds of dust formed by the time Nellie's group got on the road, choking her with fine powder. Again, she walked downwind of the slight breeze and along the edge of the dirt road. Grasshoppers jumped on her as she walked along and disturbed their resting places.

"Nellie, you can ride with us," Old Rivers called down to her.

"Thanks, but I want to walk," she said. That something stubborn in her made her want to defy the soldiers by walking as they rode along. It was a long way to the new territory, eight hundred miles or so, and she was quite sure she wouldn't walk the entire way. But for now, she wanted to walk, to turn around when she wanted and walk backward to see what she was leaving.

Old Rivers smiled at her as if he understood what was going on in her mind. He was like that. Lewis said Old Rivers could read minds, but Nellie didn't think so. She thought he read expressions on the faces of those around him that betrayed their true feelings. The way they looked away after they spoke, the falseness or genuineness of a smile, the slump of the shoulders, or the wave of a hand. Those things told what people were thinking unless they were very good at disguising their emotions.

Old Rivers sure could hide his feelings. She had never seen such an unexpressive face. The many lines told he was old, but she didn't know how old. He could be sixty or seventy or eighty, although she had never known anyone that old. The lines around his eyes showed he had smiled a lot at one time or he had squinted a lot at the sun. She had never known Old Rivers to smile, never once seen it in her twelve years on this green earth.

Maybe he didn't have reason to smile. He lived with his only son, Smoke Cloud, just the two of them. They were much alike. Both had been married, and both had lost their wives in childbirth, although many, many years apart. Etsi had told Nellie about Old Rivers once long ago when Nellie was young and didn't understand why these two men had such sad eyes and lived without a woman around.

Nellie had been inside their cabin only once—and that was on much the same type of errand that she should have run yesterday—to take an herbal medical cure to Old Rivers. He could fix most any potion better than she, Etsi said, but when a person was down with a fever, he should not have to take care of himself.

If Nellie had taken the herbs to Old Rivers yesterday, would she be the one missing today? *Where is Lewis, where is Lewis?* Her footsteps echoed the recurring thought in her mind. *Where is Lewis, where is Lewis?* The muted sound of her moccasins against the dusty earth beat the rhythm of the refrain.

She had been wearing her comfortable moccasins yesterday when the soldiers came and had never once thought of changing to her school shoes or her Sunday shoes. That was a good thing, since both pairs squeezed her feet. She had outgrown them, but she had not been fitted for new ones by the cobbler, a Cherokee who had recently opened a shop in town. He made heavy shoes like white people wore, not the lightweight moccasins that any Cherokee woman with some good hide and a quill needle could make.

Nellie could make moccasins, but she didn't have the skill or quickness that Etsi had. If she walked the entire way to the new territory, she would probably need another pair of moccasins. Edoda would have to kill a deer or cow along the way. Or would the soldiers have shoes for all the Cherokee?

She walked along, kicking up more dust, twirling around to see the world behind her, see to the side, see everything. She wanted to memorize every blade of green grass, every crook in the trunk of every tree, every bird that sang its song from the branches of the trees. She bent down and touched the earth, just to feel the land of her forefathers.

The sun was not yet straight up when a soldier yelled, "Hold up!"

In the distance, Nellie saw hundreds and hundreds of Cherokee. Wagons were lined up along the log walls of a stockade. Campfires blazed for cooking in the warmth of the June sun.

A soldier rode out from the stockade. "Take them over this way!" he shouted. "Past this stockade! We'll put this group near the river." He rode along their wagon train, pointing his finger at people and moving his lips silently, obviously counting them.

"Why aren't they going inside?" a nearby soldier asked.

"There's no more room," said the soldier doing the counting. "The campgrounds run from stockade to stockade for forty miles. We'll have to guard them outside. Harder for us, but they know the law. They know they have no choice but to relocate."

CHAPTER 4
The Stockade

As their caravan passed the open door of the stockade, Nellie glanced inside. Quite a few roofed cabins squatted along the sides, but there weren't nearly enough for the number of Cherokee the stockade kept prisoner.

Hundreds, no, thousands were camped near the stockade, Nellie estimated as her wagon train passed more and more Cherokee. She wrinkled her nose at the smell. Were there no outhouses around? Here she was, forced from her home by soldiers with guns, and all she could think about was how to relieve herself!

"We have tents and food," one soldier told another soldier near Nellie, "but the Indians are refusing both. What's wrong with these people? I've never seen so many people be so quiet."

"Quiet?" Nellie murmured. The noises she heard were low murmurs broken by sobs. Her people stood, squatted, walked, and tended to others lying on the ground.

"Lewis?" Etsi rose from her seat on the wagon, hope in her voice. She held onto the lurching wagon with one hand, her other hand outstretched as if reaching for him.

Nellie saw the boy Etsi had called to, but when he turned around, he was not Lewis. He walked like Lewis, and he wore a black hat like Lewis, but it was not her brother.

Etsi collapsed on the seat, her face contorted in agony—not physical pain but a much deeper emotional pain. Where was Lewis?

It was a while before the lead wagon stopped. The one after that went to the next area past the first one; the next one went a little farther and stopped, until the entire line of wagons was halted.

As soon as the oxen were staked out to graze, the fire was built for cooking, and water was carried from the creek, Edoda said, "I'm going to look for Lewis. He's got to be among all these people."

"I'll look, too," Nellie said.

Edoda took her hand. "Good. Two of us will cover twice the territory, but mark where we are so you can find your way back here. We don't want to lose you, too."

"I'll count wagons until we reach the stockade," Nellie said. "That will be our number, and I won't forget." Together they walked back toward the stockade. As soon as they reached wagons that weren't in their group, Edoda asked if anyone had seen Lewis Starr and described him. While he was talking with that group, Nellie went to the next, and they crisscrossed, hopping from campfire to campfire, spreading the word about Lewis.

They also were given a long list of others to look for as they scouted through the camp. Fathers who were hunting or in far fields when the soldiers came were left to be rounded up by other soldiers. Other children on errands at the mill or in town were thought to be with other groups.

Since the campfires weren't in a long row but were spread out, Nellie soon lost sight of Edoda. But that didn't stop her from continuing on her quest.

"Morning Sun," she called when she saw a friend from the mission school.

"Nellie, when did you get here?"

"Just a few minutes ago, but my brother Lewis isn't with us. Have you seen him?"

Morning Sun shook her head, her long dark braids whipping back and forth. "We have been here two days, and I've not seen him yet."

Nellie described what had happened the day before, and Morning Sun gave an account of their roundup. "Like cattle," she said, "except one soldier was very nice. He kept saying what a shame this was to make us leave our land and that it wasn't right."

"That doesn't help," Nellie said. "We're over past the stockade. I counted eighty-four wagons. We're eighty-five. Come over later. I'll be back there after we find Lewis."

"Which way are you going? I'll search the other way," Morning Sun offered.

They went in opposite directions, each shouting for Lewis as they walked.

Nellie saw other girls she knew from school. Dancing Wind, Green Leaf, Night Wind, and Annie. Nellie had once asked Etsi why she had an English name and not a Cherokee name. She was told the Starrs felt that if their children had English names, they would better fit into this new world that mixed the white men and the Cherokee.

"If you wish a Cherokee name, it can be earned," Etsi had said. Nellie had no idea what name she would earn. What would be her strength? Or what would she remind others of? So far, she had remained plain Nellie. Her friend Annie was called Flower Petal in Cherokee, but she went by Annie.

"Edoda!" Nellie called when she saw her father a few wagons away. "Nothing?"

He held out his hands, palms up. "No one has seen him. I've not been in the stockade. Have you?"

"No."

They went inside together, with Nellie explaining to the soldier at the gate that they were looking for Lewis. Once inside, they split up and went along different walls.

The stench of human and animal waste was much worse inside where the wind couldn't blow it away. The heat was more oppressive, too. Nellie was thankful their wagon train had arrived later and they weren't contained within the fortification.

She and Edoda each covered half the enormous area. Nellie saw sickness everywhere. Mostly the sick were elderly, but there were also many children lying down under the shade of a few tents. Several times, she heard the whooping sound of a cough, and fear gripped her for those who had the dreaded disease. She scurried from group to group, mostly looking, not asking questions about Lewis. An hour later, when she met Edoda at the gate, neither one had seen him.

"We must get back to Etsi," Edoda said. "He may have been directed to our camp."

Nellie didn't think that was likely, but she was hungry. Starving, really, and from the looks of the Cherokee around her, they felt the same way. Many had no campfires lit for cooking but sat around charred remnants of earlier fires.

"Why haven't the soldiers given them food?" Nellie asked her father as they hurried toward their campsite.

"I've heard that many are refusing food offered by the white men. Their pride will not allow them to take food from those who take our land."

Nellie could understand that pride, but her growling stomach would not have held out if she walked past a soldier handing out food.

"Lewis?" Etsi called from her kneeling position beside the stew pot. She looked beyond Nellie and Edoda, obviously hoping to spot Lewis.

"Nothing yet," Edoda said.

"We'll find him," Nellie said with false cheerfulness.

"He will come to the camp." Old Rivers sat on the ground, leaning against the wheel of his wagon, which was pulled directly behind the Starr wagon.

"How are you feeling?" Nellie asked. She squatted on the grass beside him, drawn to him because his words promised that Lewis would show up. How he knew that, she didn't know, but he sounded so confident, so sure that it would be so.

"I'll be fine with a little more time," he said.

"You speak strong words," she said, probing—without asking outright—to find out why he was certain that Lewis would show up.

"Yes, they are strong words, and they will be kept. Lewis is a smart boy." He must have seen something change in Nellie's eyes for he immediately added, "He is smart in the ways of a hunter. You are smart in the ways of book learning. Both ways are smart ways." He coughed as if speaking so many words had worn him out.

Nellie lifted her eyebrows. What did Old Rivers know about her? She had not been around him much and could never recall a private conversation with him.

"Lewis is proud you are his sister with your gift of languages."

"Lewis is proud of *me?*" she asked.

"Of course. And you should be proud of him."

Nellie tried to think why. He was a boy full of mischief, and he didn't value the things she held dear.

"His common sense is from the heart, not the mind, and he knows what's important," Old Rivers said, and again he was racked with a tight cough.

"But he's not quite twelve," Nellie said.

"Many things are learned at a young age. Wisdom is gained by time, but knowledge can come early."

"The stew is ready," Etsi said. This time she had dug out some dishes so that the Starr family and Old Rivers and his son could eat at the same time. "We don't know how long we'll be here before we go to the new land, and we will eat like the civilized people we are."

We may be civilized, Nellie thought, *but we have no table, just bowls and spoons.* But they had more than the Cherokee at the next campfire, who ate from hollowed gourd bowls. Again she was reminded of what a privileged upbringing she had. Having a nice house, more food, and more book learning didn't make her better than the Cherokee at the next campfire. It might have made her life easier, but they were all in the same place now. All feeling the same sense of loss.

Edoda asked a blessing for the food they were about to receive and added a plea for Lewis to be found.

"But he is not lost," Old Rivers muttered softly so that only Nellie heard him.

Nellie glanced at him, then at Smoke Cloud, his son. Smoke Cloud rarely said much, and his look was always a haunted stare.

He is lonely, Nellie decided, and she made up her mind to talk to him on this trip to the new country.

After they had eaten, Edoda went off to look for Lewis again. Nellie and Sarah helped Etsi wipe the dishes. When the dishes were put away in an easy-to-get-to spot in the wagon, Nellie sat in the grass beside Smoke Cloud. Old Rivers had fallen asleep on the shaded grass under their wagon after drinking another of Etsi's potions.

"Do you think it is useless to look for Lewis?" Nellie asked.

"He will come when he is ready." He spoke with the same authority as Old Rivers.

"What do you think he's doing? And how will he find us?"

"He can follow any tracks, animal's or man's," Smoke Cloud said, his eyes brightening with pride. "So many wagons have left him a path he could follow with his eyes closed."

"Did you teach him how to track?" Nellie asked.

He nodded with a slight smile.

Edoda returned to camp with the news that he had spoken to Reverend Jesse Bushyhead, who was one of the best Cherokee preachers around.

"Did Jesse have any news of Lewis?" Etsi asked.

"Nothing, but I am coming to believe Old Rivers is right. Lewis will find us, not the other way around. But I have much news."

He sat on the tongue of the wagon and talked. "Some of these people have been here for weeks. There has been much sickness in the stockade, and some of the old have died from disease. Three children have also died, and many are weak from starvation. I have talked to some men and tried to make them change their minds about not taking food from the white soldiers."

"I would take food," Sarah said.

"Yes, you would," Edoda agreed. "I'd see to it. The white man's government will provide for us as they promised. I hate what has happened to us as much as any man here, but the Cherokee way is to know when the past is gone."

"That is so," Old Rivers said. His voice startled Nellie, who thought he was asleep. But he was awake with his ears open, even if his eyes were closed. "We are no longer caretakers of the past. We must build on what has gone before."

"We will take the best of the Cherokee ways with us," Edoda said, "and the best of the white man's ways. We must leave what is bad behind us."

"Did you learn when we are to start on the journey?" Etsi asked.

"A group leaves tomorrow, but we will not be part of it. There are rumors that other groups will be delayed."

"Till when?" Nellie asked.

"Until a break in the weather. The drought has lowered the rivers, and water travel is near impossible. Tomorrow's group will be the last to make it if the water falls any lower. And on the overland route, springs are drying up. Too many here lie sick of bilious fever and whooping cough, and the white government may let us stay until the weather breaks."

"But who knows when that will be?" Etsi asked no one in particular.

"No one knows," Old Rivers said. "No one knows."

CHAPTER 5

What Happened to Lewis

"May I go see Morning Sun?" Nellie asked Etsi. "I can keep an eye out for Lewis."

"You may go, but be back here to help with supper."

As she walked through the huge encampment toward Morning Sun's wagon, Nellie glanced around, looking for the black hat that Lewis would never be without. It was much like Edoda's black hat but without the crow feather that distinguished Edoda's.

"Morning Sun," Nellie called when she spotted her friend sitting under the wagon's shade.

"Did you find your brother?" Morning Sun jumped up and rushed to Nellie's side.

"No, but we trust he will find us. Want to walk around?"

Morning Sun checked with her mother, and then the two girls walked around the camp, looking for other friends.

As they passed the entrance to the stockade, Morning Sun said, "It is our good fortune that we are here. We've heard that at other camps everyone must stay inside the stockade."

"How can they get so many people inside?"

"They are crowded so close there is barely room to stand," Morning Sun said. "So we hear."

Nellie hoped it wasn't true. If the soldiers here forced everyone inside, there would be even more sickness.

"Oh, no." Nellie stepped back. Four men carrying a wooden

coffin walked somberly toward the open stockade gate. "Let's go," she whispered.

"At least that person will be buried on Cherokee land. They've started a cemetery over yonder." Morning Sun pointed toward the north edge of the woods that encroached on the campgrounds.

With heads bowed in respect, the girls backed away from the grieving family who followed the coffin. Clouds covered the sun, casting a shadow over the group.

"Has this happened before?" Nellie asked.

A woman standing nearby answered, "It happens many times every day. This sickness season and the heat are too much for the old—and the young."

"I think we can add heartbreak to that," Nellie said. In her wanderings in the camp, she had seen no happy faces on the elders, no smiles at all, just heads lowered in grief. Only very young children seemed unperturbed by the situation, and their laughter as they played seemed out of place among such a sad group of people.

The girls walked toward the edge of the camp as the late afternoon breeze picked up and blew Nellie's long black hair into her eyes. She pulled it back and glanced up. Clouds were moving in. Dark clouds moving fast. Lightning streaked the sky, and thunder boomed.

"I'd better get back to the others," she said. She left Morning Sun at her campsite, then ran to her area, arriving only moments before the sky let loose and rain drenched the land. She huddled with the others under their wagon.

The downpour lasted a brief ten minutes before the storm clouds scudded toward the east. The western sun shone brightly again, turning a freshly washed, glistening world into one where

Nellie thought she might actually see steam rising from the ground.

"That might help the drought," Nellie said.

"It's not enough," Edoda said. "We need a steady rain for many hours. But we do need shelter from more rain, since we'll be here for some time."

"Lewis is somewhere in the rain," Etsi said.

Nellie didn't know what to reply.

"We will ask about a tent, or we'll make a brush shelter," Edoda said. "Once everything is dry. And we'll make an outhouse, too."

"Away from our camp," Nellie said. The stench from improper sewage had only intensified since the downpour.

"As far away as we're allowed," Edoda said. He glanced toward the soldiers patrolling the outer perimeters of the campground.

The brief rainstorm made things miserable. Nellie wiped sweat from her forehead and wished she could slip down to the creek for a bath. She was still in the same dress she'd worn yesterday morning when the soldiers had come. Was it just yesterday that her world had been turned upside down and inside out?

She wondered if she could get to the trunk where her writing supplies were kept. She asked Etsi, who helped her rummage around in the wagon until they unloaded enough things to get to the trunk. With her pen and ink and paper, she sat on the tailgate of the wagon and used the wooden box of dishes as a desk. She poured her heart out in her journal, starting with the very moment she had heard the soldiers were coming. She wrote about missing Lewis and the pain of leaving home.

"Lewis!" Sarah screamed.

Nellie looked up to see Lewis riding his pony and pulling a

heavily laden travois. The two poles of his travois left a trail in the soft wet earth.

"Need some more paper, Nellie?" he asked.

Nellie dropped her writing, jumped off the wagon, and joined the family rushing for Lewis.

"Lewis! Lewis!" Etsi pulled him off his horse and held him close. Edoda didn't wait his turn but hugged him from the back, putting his arms around Lewis and encompassing Etsi, too.

Tears washed Etsi's face, and Nellie found herself wiping tears of joy. Sarah jumped up and down beside Lewis. Old Rivers and Smoke Cloud joined the group.

"I knew you would find us," Smoke Cloud said. "Just a matter of when."

"Where have you been?" Nellie asked.

"Where were you when the soldiers came?" Sarah asked at the same time.

"Give him a minute," Etsi said. "Do you need water? Are you hungry?"

"Both—water and food," Lewis said. "And for Blaze."

"I'll get fresh cool water," Nellie said and grabbed the nearly empty bucket from its hook on the side of the wagon. "Not a word until I get back. Promise?"

"Let's get him fixed up," Edoda said. "Then we'll listen to his story."

Edoda unhooked Blaze from the travois, took off the saddle, and led the pony toward the creek. He walked alongside Nellie. She glanced over her shoulder and saw Lewis kneeling beside Old Rivers. Smoke Cloud stood, talking to Lewis. Etsi and Sarah were building up the fire to start supper.

"Where do you think he's been?" Nellie asked.

"He will tell us in his time," Edoda said. "I thank God that he is with us now."

"I hope he is safe with us, but he may have been safer away from this camp," Nellie said. As she dipped the bucket in the cool water, she told Edoda of the funeral march she had seen. Blaze drank his fill a few feet farther downstream.

"I know there is much sickness, and we must stay away from the sick ones unless they have no family to care for them."

"At least the dead one is lying in Cherokee land," Nellie echoed the words Morning Sun had spoken earlier.

"We spring from this earth—our hearts and spirits, and it is good that the departed one can return to it. But the rest of us must go on and claim a new land. And now Lewis will be going with us to the new territory."

"Yes. I wonder what he meant by asking if I needed more paper."

"We'll find out soon enough. Blaze, that is enough water for now." With a tug on the reins, Edoda gently pulled up the pony's head and led him away from the stream.

They hurried back to the camp, where Lewis was still being fussed over by Etsi. Nellie filled the dipper with fresh water and handed it to Lewis, who drank it, then filled it again.

"Now can you tell us where you've been?" Nellie asked. "Or must we wait for supper?"

Etsi's wide smile stretched across her face. She seemed unable to stop smiling, and Nellie loved seeing her mother so happy.

"We will cook after we hear of his adventures," Etsi said.

They gathered in a circle near Old Rivers's wagon where there was no hot cook fire to make the steamy heat more unbearable.

Nellie sat on the ground next to Sarah and across from Lewis so she could hear his every word. Beside Lewis was the travois laid flat, a blanket covering lumpy items.

Lewis started his story with a confession. "When I left Old Rivers's place, I didn't go directly home."

"Nothing out of the ordinary there," Nellie said, and they all laughed.

"I was riding in the woods, thinking I'd hunt some game for supper," he said. "I was near the road but hidden by the trees, and I saw the soldiers ride by. Of course, I knew why they had come."

"Didn't you want to go with us?" Sarah asked.

"Of course I wanted to go with you," Lewis said, "but I thought I'd see what their plan was before I made myself known. I saw Nellie drag a trunk to the front porch, and that gave me the idea to ride to the store to get supplies we would need." He took off his black hat and wiped his brow.

"That's why you asked if I wanted more paper?" Nellie asked.

"Yes. I brought you paper from Edoda's store. There were no workers in the store, and already people were running in, just taking what they wanted, so I did the same." He reached under the blanket beside him and pulled out a stack of papers.

"All food was gone before I got there, but I got other things. For you, Sarah," he said and reached under the blanket again, "I got this cornstalk doll."

"Oooh," Sarah squealed. "Now I have two dolls. They can play together." She jumped up from her place in the circle, ran to the wagon, and proudly held both dolls in her lap when she sat down.

"For you, Etsi, I grabbed some cloth that had been trampled

on. It's a little dirty." He pulled a bundle of bright blue fabric from his pile of surprises.

"It's lovely, Lewis. Thank you. It just needs a washing, and then I'll make a new dress. Thank you." Etsi reached over and kissed Lewis on the forehead.

"Was the store overrun?" Edoda asked.

Lewis looked down at the ground as if studying it for words. "It was ransacked. Shelves were torn down. Aisles were strewn with things that weren't already taken." He reached under the blanket. "But for you, Edoda, I have. . ." He paused for effect, looked around, and then whispered, "Your ax." He raised a blanket corner where the handle could be seen.

"My ax!" Edoda said softly. He glanced at the soldier on patrol nearly a hundred feet away. "Weapons aren't allowed."

Lewis grinned sheepishly. "I left it under the tree where I was chopping wood two days ago, but this time, that was a good thing. It will be good to have it in the new place."

"It sure will," Edoda said. "We'll just keep it our secret."

Lewis nodded and reached under his blanket again. "For you, Smoke Cloud, I have your arrowheads." He produced a leather bag full of Smoke Cloud's fine work.

"You went back to our house?" Smoke Cloud asked.

"I went there after I got the few things left at the store. You were already gone and had been in quite a hurry, from the looks of all you left. I gathered supplies and used your workshop to make my travois to carry things. I didn't like the idea of riding around carrying a doll," he said with a laugh. "I was in the outbuilding when white looters came. But they didn't see me. I put as many tools on the travois as it could carry."

"You did good work," Old Rivers said. "Smart boy."

"I have something for you, too," Lewis said. "You did not bring your treasure."

Old Rivers sat up straight; his eyes filled with wonder. "I did not think."

"My edoda is sick," Smoke Cloud said. "I sat him on the wagon, and I packed, and I did not remember."

"You told me once that your treasure lay behind the stone that moves. I pulled and pounded on every stone in the chimney until I found the one." He pulled a small pouch from his pocket.

Old Rivers took it in shaky hands. Slowly he pulled the string that tied it shut, and then he shook the bag until something shiny dropped into his hand.

"What is it?" Nellie asked.

"I don't know," Lewis said. "I didn't look."

Old Rivers did not answer but stared at his hand.

"It is a cross of pure gold," Smoke Cloud said. "It belonged to my etsi."

"Pure gold?" Nellie asked.

"When my edoda found gold flakes in the creek, he saved them until he had a good amount, and he had this made for my etsi. She wore it always."

"It is indeed a treasure," Etsi said. "It was treasured by Moon Silver because it was given in love. It is treasured by Old Rivers because she loved it so."

Old Rivers put his shaky hand on Lewis's shoulder. "Thank you for remembering."

Lewis nodded with a beaming smile. "I have also brought your farm tools." He flicked the blanket from one side of the travois to reveal a hoe, a rake, a saw, and a small one-horse plow. "Men were at our house, so I could not save ours," Lewis told Edoda.

"Thank you for our tools," Smoke Cloud said. "I was not allowed out to the shed. I was fortunate to get the few things I could grab before we were forced onto the road."

Edoda, Lewis, and Smoke Cloud loaded the tools onto Old Rivers's wagon. Nellie and Sarah helped Etsi build up the fire for the stew of boiling greens and ham, thickened with finely ground cornmeal.

The evening meal was a festive occasion with the family whole again. Edoda asked the blessing and thanked God for returning his son. After they had eaten and cleaned up, the entire Starr family walked to the evening worship service held by Reverend Jesse Bushyhead.

Several preachers were in their midst, but the Starr family knew Reverend Bushyhead, who rode a preaching circuit and had come to town several times to hold camp meetings.

His worship service was similar to those meetings. He called the Cherokee to come to the Lord. He called for the Cherokee to free their slaves, and he drew a straight line to the treatment of the Cherokee by white men and the treatment of black slaves by both the Cherokee and the whites.

Nellie didn't know if his preaching did any good on that point. Many slaves stayed with their masters in the camp. Morning Sun's family had three slaves who helped in the fields and one who helped out in the house. The slaves were going to the new land to help there. As far as Nellie knew, Morning Sun's slaves were treated well, just like family. But enslavement was enslavement. And she agreed with Reverend Bushyhead. It was wrong.

CHAPTER 6

The Long Summer

Early the next morning, Reverend Bushyhead held morning service, and the Starr family attended. Somehow, Reverend Bushyhead had managed to pack several hymnals written in the Cherokee language, so the voices of at least a hundred Cherokee people united in harmonious worship. Their songs did not compete with the songs of birds, which had mostly deserted the area of the large camp that spread out around the fortification.

Etsi stood in a line to get food rations from the soldiers, and meals were prepared over the open fire. Nellie was tired of the same old stew, but without a cookstove, baking was impossible.

"We must go back to the old ways of cooking," Old Rivers said. He showed Etsi how to make an oven by heating a pot and turning it sideways in the fire and closing up the opening to keep the heat inside. Cornbread was added to the meals.

The days fell into a pattern. By late morning, the sun scorched the earth, and by afternoon the heat drained the energy from even the adventuresome Lewis. The water level in the Hiwassee River dropped, and the rumor Edoda had heard of no more wagon trains west until the weather broke became true.

"We must prepare for a long summer," Edoda said. The government hadn't provided enough tents for all the Cherokee, and he had gotten permission from the soldiers to build a hut to live in until the next batch of travelers were sent to Indian Territory.

"A house, like our old house?" Sarah asked.

"Not at all. This will be a simple brush shack that will shelter us from the harsh heat of the summer sun and from the rain, if we are so fortunate as to get another shower."

Lewis enthusiastically helped saw straight limbs, using the tools he had rescued from Old Rivers's tool shed. Nellie dragged limbs to the area beside their wagon and held them upright while Edoda drove them in the ground to form two rows a foot apart. Between the rows, they stuffed limbs with leaves and dry grasses. The roof was made of poles with limbs interwoven between them.

"It's like the hideout the boys and I made in the woods," Lewis said, "except we used standing trees for the walls."

"Since we don't have any trees close to the wagon," said Edoda, "this will do nicely. Nellie, would you carry that heavy pot for your mother?"

The pot was no heavier than normal, and Etsi had managed it many times, but Nellie hurried to help.

Edoda and Etsi exchanged a look that Nellie didn't understand.

"What is it?" Nellie asked Etsi. "What's wrong?"

"Nothing is wrong," Etsi said and cast a quick glance at Edoda. He nodded, and she said, "We'll talk about this tonight."

They finished the shelter by late afternoon. It wasn't large, merely some eight feet by eight feet, and it was fully enclosed only on three sides with about half the fourth side closed, leaving a wide doorway. It gave a place to sit and sleep for the five Starrs. They unloaded a few things from the wagon for easy access during the day. The dishes and cooking utensils were stored in one corner. Blankets to be used as mattresses were piled in another corner.

After supper and another evening service, which was becoming the routine, Nellie asked Etsi to explain what she had meant earlier.

"Let's all go in the hut," Etsi said, "and prepare for bed. Then we'll talk."

Nellie knew Etsi was about to say something important, and she quickly spread out the bedding.

"Hurry, Lewis. Sarah, lie down," Nellie said.

As soon as they were all lying quietly in the dark, with only the flicker from fireflies around them and the dying campfire for light, Nellie said, "Etsi?"

"I'm going to have a baby," Etsi said. "You'll have a brother or sister."

"Wonderful," Sarah said. "A real baby to play with!"

"When?" Nellie asked. "Is it well?"

"In the winter. Around Christmas," Etsi said, but she did not answer Nellie's second question.

"She will be a Christmas gift," Sarah said.

"Or he," Lewis said. "I could use a brother. We have two girls, but I'm the only boy."

"Please, is it a girl, Etsi?" Sarah asked.

"No one can tell you before it's born," Etsi said. "But whichever it is, it will be God's miracle given to us in the new land."

"We will all help you," Nellie said. "Won't we?"

"Yes, we'll do everything," Lewis said in a strong voice, and Nellie thought he remembered three years ago as well as she.

"I can help, too," Sarah said in her lilting way. From Sarah's tone of voice, Nellie was just as sure that she did not remember what had happened. Sarah would have been just two when Etsi had given birth to a tiny little girl. The baby had come early, and she had died just minutes after the birth. Etsi had cried. Nellie had cried. When the midwife sent Nellie in search of Edoda and Lewis, who had gone outside, she found them both with red eyes and wet cheeks.

"This baby will be fine," Edoda said. "He will bring with him a new beginning for our family."

"He?" Etsi's tone was as light as Sarah's. "You are so sure we will have another son?"

"I have a good chance of being right," Edoda said. Nellie heard him kiss Etsi in the darkness. "And he will be fine."

The next morning at breakfast, Sarah told Old Rivers and Smoke Cloud about the baby.

Smoke Cloud looked away from Etsi, but Old Rivers spoke up. "This is good. Very good. It makes us look to the future. All of us were born in this land, soon to be our old land. The new one will be born in the new land. That will be a new beginning."

"You and Edoda speak the same words," Nellie said.

"Both are very wise," Smoke Cloud said.

The day stretched out much the same as the day before. And the day after was the same. Waiting, always waiting.

Lewis played near the wagon because he was not allowed to hunt with his bow and arrow. He had hidden it on the travois but could not reveal it in case the soldiers took it away. Each day, he gathered firewood. Sarah carried her two dolls around and played much to herself. Nellie was allowed to see Morning Sun, but she was the only friend who came to the area. Etsi was very afraid that the sicknesses that were everywhere would come to her family, and she wanted her children near her and away from the sick ones.

One of Nellie's chores was carrying the heavy water bucket, and she was dismayed when day after day she saw the water line go lower and lower. She and Etsi cooked for the family and Old Rivers and Smoke Cloud. The two Cherokee men soon seemed like members of their family.

Edoda learned that his sisters and their families were in other stockades. Etsi's parents and brothers and sisters were in still different stockades. They heard reports from time to time that the conditions elsewhere matched the conditions in their camp.

Death and dying were constant companions. The graveyard on the edge of the campground grew. One morning, Nellie and Morning Sun counted ten burials. Even more dead were buried in the afternoon. Reverend Bushyhead conducted many of the ceremonies, but sometimes a shaman led a funeral procession.

Etsi frowned when Nellie told her they had watched a shaman shake his rattle and lead a grieving family to the cemetery.

"Let's not dwell on the funerals," Etsi said. "You need to help me with herb gathering."

The soldiers who guarded the camp perimeters let them go to the woods with a canvas bag to gather greens to boil and herbs for cooking and healing. Morning Sun followed behind Nellie, who walked behind Etsi.

"I'm not sure what we're looking for," Morning Sun said.

"Just pick when Etsi says to pick. Or scrape bark. Or dig root," Nellie said over her shoulder.

Etsi stopped here and there, and the girls picked greens and stuffed them in the bag. They collected cedar bark to mix with oils to make a potion that would keep bugs from biting, a necessary thing since the putrid smells of death and the unsanitary conditions in the camp brought flying insects by the thousands.

"This looks like something we need," Morning Sun called from a nearby clearing. "Huckleberries."

In the midst of the woods in a small area free of trees grew a huckleberry patch.

"Etsi, we'll pick some berries," Nellie called to her etsi, who had headed in a different direction into the woods.

"Good," Etsi said. "We can have them for supper."

Nellie loved the sweet blue berries and picked some for her bag but ate more than she saved. The low bushes were heavily laden, and she was surprised that they had not already been picked by other Cherokee—but perhaps the soldiers had not let others outside their pickets.

She dropped to her knees and crawled among the berry bushes. She was so intent on eating the sweet berries, it took her a moment to smell something that made her freeze.

Cucumbers! Etsi raised them in the garden, and Nellie knew them well, but this was not the good smell of a vegetable. This was the smell of a copperhead.

Only her eyes moved as she searched the ground ahead that the low bushes didn't cover.

"Nellie!" Morning Sun called from a distance of several feet.

"Stay there!" Nellie whispered. "A snake!"

A movement caught her eye. It was not just one snake that Nellie had disturbed, but a nest of copperheads, six of them. And they were not on the ground ahead of her; they were inches from her left hand, which rested on the earth beside a bush. She was amazed that her brain counted the snakes because her heart pounded so loudly she could hear it in her ears.

Ever so slowly, she backed away, leaving her hands in place, bracing herself. One knee, then the other, another few inches. Slowly, slowly. She moved her right hand and was pushing off with her left hand when a snake latched onto her hand below her little finger.

She stood up and backed out of the thicket of huckleberry bushes with the snake attached to her hand, its fangs sunk into her flesh. She grabbed its head, forced it off, and threw it on the ground.

"Etsi! Etsi!" she screamed.

"Nellie! Are you all right?" Morning Sun stood rooted to a spot in another thicket of bushes. "Where is it?"

"I've been bit. Back out. Now!"

But Morning Sun didn't move. Her eyes were huge, and the color drained from her face.

"Etsi!" Nellie called again to her mother. She had lost sight of her when they had started picking berries. "Etsi!"

"Nellie?" Etsi called and ran from the woods toward her. "What is it?"

"A copperhead bit me."

"Nellie! Where?"

"In the bushes. There's a whole nest of them."

Etsi had nearly reached her now. "Where?"

"Oh!" Nellie realized what her etsi meant. "My hand." With her right hand, she squeezed her left wrist, trying to keep the poison from spreading, trying to keep it in her hand. Already her hand was swollen around the bite.

"Put your hand down," Etsi said. "Walk slowly. Calm your heart."

But how could she calm her heart? That was impossible. Or was it?

She closed her eyes. "Please calm my heart," she prayed. "God, please calm my heart."

"Morning Sun!" Etsi called. "Help me. We must carry her."

Morning Sun finally moved swiftly out of the bushes.

"No!" Nellie cried. "The baby."

"It is fine," Etsi said. "Nellie, hold your hand on your stomach. Morning Sun, grab her feet. I'll get her shoulders."

Between the two of them, they managed to get Nellie in a flat position and carried her out of the thicket and into the woods toward the camp. With each heartbeat, Nellie felt the poison move up her arm, and it hurt so bad, it felt as if someone was hitting her arm with a stick. Another heartbeat, another inch higher the poison moved, another hit on her arm with a stick.

"Help! Help!" Etsi yelled, and Morning Sun screamed, "Help!"

A soldier rode his horse toward them. "What happened?" he asked as he dismounted.

"A copperhead bit her," Etsi said in Cherokee, but the soldier shook his head as if he didn't understand.

"Nellie, tell him," Etsi said.

Nellie was feeling faint, but she said, "Snakebite. My hand."

"Rattler?" he asked as he stooped and took Nellie from Etsi and Morning Sun.

"Copperhead," Nellie answered.

"Good," he said. "Not so much poison." He motioned for Etsi to hold his horse still, and he laid Nellie across the saddle, her head hanging off one side of the horse and her legs off the other. He mounted and sat behind the saddle. "Put your hand down."

Nellie obeyed, letting her left arm dangle while holding on to a stirrup with her right hand. Her chin bounced against the saddle as the horse took off at a good pace, and she turned her head and tried to hold it still. She could see Etsi and Morning Sun running after them.

"We're almost there," the soldier said in a few minutes.

He had taken her to the soldiers' headquarters. "We'll have Doc take a look at you."

"God, please calm my heart," Nellie whispered as the soldier carried her to a tent.

"Copperhead bite," he announced as he laid her on a cot. "Hand."

The doctor looked at her hand, poked around the two puncture holes from the fangs, and smoothed on some salve. He held his fingers on the pulse in her wrist. "Slow heartbeat. Good." Then he wrapped her entire arm from her shoulder all the way to her hand with a bandage.

"Just stay still," he said. "Looks like more venom than usual, but you'll be just fine."

Edoda and Etsi appeared at the tent opening as the doctor finished with Nellie.

"Take her home?" Edoda asked.

Home? Nellie thought. She could not go home again, and Edoda was surely not calling their little brushy hut by the wagon their home.

"She needs to be still," the doctor said. "She can stay here awhile, but if you want to carry her, you can take her to your place."

"Carry me?" Nellie asked.

"Yes," Edoda said.

He scooped her up and carried her past wagon after wagon to the Starr camp. Etsi kept up a constant chatter beside her. Morning Sun, Lewis, Sarah, Old Rivers, and Smoke Cloud surrounded her as soon as Edoda laid her on a blanket inside the hut.

"Want some water?" Lewis asked.

"Does it hurt?" Sarah asked.

"I'll be fine," Nellie assured them, but her hand stung and felt numb at the same time. It looked like the paw of a cat, with no separation of the fingers.

She did not find the enforced rest an easy time. She wanted to be helping Etsi with the chores. She wanted to walk with Morning Sun. But she stayed still for several days, and the swelling went away. She was left with only two scars as a memory of the copperhead's fangs.

As soon as she was up and about, the days fell into a different pattern. Hot and hotter, dry and dryer, waiting and waiting longer.

June quickly turned into a hotter July. Edoda told the family that Principle Chief John Ross had negotiated with the white government to let the Cherokee be in charge of their own removal. They would hire merchants to supply them with blankets and food along the trail. And the Cherokee police, the Light Horse, would keep order.

The plan was made. Around thirteen thousand people would be divided into groups of about a thousand each to make the journey.

"Which group will we be in?" Lewis asked.

"I don't know," Edoda said.

"When will we go?" Nellie asked.

"Not until autumn. Not until there is a break in the weather," Edoda said.

July turned into August. The council, lead by Chief John Ross, decided it was time to prepare. The first group left near the end of the month. The second group left the first of September. Then it was time for the third group to depart.

"We are in the third group, led by Reverend Bushyhead," Edoda told them. "It is time to go."

CHAPTER 7

The Journey Begins

On September third, the Bushyhead group—950 men, women, and children—departed from Rattlesnake Spring. Edoda had retrieved Nellie's black pony from the soldiers but not Sarah's, and Nellie rode alongside the wagon. Lewis rode Blaze near Old Rivers's wagon, which fell in line right behind the Starr wagon.

As they started off, a cry was heard, a low moan coming from the women. Young children waved good-bye to the mountains. Nellie felt tears slide down her cheeks, and she made no move to stop them but merely turned her face away from her family so they wouldn't see her cry. She wanted to be brave, to be a proud Cherokee, to be a person who could look forward to change instead of mourning the past.

But it felt so wrong, so very wrong, that the white men were taking their land, her father's business, and their wonderful home with her room overlooking the long lane to the house. The white government promised to pay the displaced Cherokee for their losses when they reached the new land, but Nellie wondered how they would measure the loss of her heart. She had sat by that window in her bedroom and looked out on the distant mountains and dreamed of the day she would have a home and family of her own. She had gazed at the lower foothills and the green pastures, at the trees swaying with the wind, and she had listened to the birds sing their happy songs, and at night the. . .

A sob broke from her throat, and for a moment she held her hand to her mouth to keep more sobs inside.

This was the trail where her people cried. She glanced at the wagon and saw Etsi cover her face with her hands. A tear rolled down Edoda's cheek. In the next wagon, she saw Old Rivers sitting tall and proud, his head held erect as he gazed straight ahead. But there was a tear on his cheek, as well. This truly was the trail where even the strong men like Edoda and Old Rivers showed how their hearts were broken by leaving their homeland.

She lifted her hand in farewell to the mountains, to the sky, to the trees, to the earth where her parents had played as children and her grandparents had played as children and their grandparents before them.

"Good-bye," she whispered. "Good-bye." She turned her head to the front and followed the ponies ahead of her. John Deerborn was three wagons ahead, and she wiped her tears and nudged Midnight forward.

John looked as bad as she felt, and she could tell he was struggling not to cry while she was beside him.

"Let's keep a sharp eye out for eagles before we get too far out of the mountain regions," she said. "We must look to the future. We'll find some feathers for you to pass down to your grandson."

He sighed, a huge sigh from deep inside.

"You are right," he said. "Our grandparents are our past and our future. They are what we hope to become someday. So I will look for feathers to give to my grandson."

"The wagons roll so slowly, we could ride off if we saw any likely places for an aerie and easily catch up with them later."

"You are right again," he said. A hint of a smile just tugging at the edges of his mouth showed that he had turned his mind from sorrow to hope.

"Call for me anytime you spot a place we could look," she said and turned Midnight out of the way of the wagons to wait for her parents.

"Anything you need, Etsi?" she asked when they pulled alongside her and she urged Midnight forward again.

"No, nothing," her etsi said, but there was a catch in her voice, and Nellie could see her eyes were red from crying.

The wagon jostled and creaked as it rolled along the trail. Maybe riding her pony would be easier on Etsi and the unborn baby, but when Nellie suggested it, Etsi waved it aside.

"I am where I need to be now," she said. She rested her arm on Edoda's shoulder, and Nellie figured she needed the comfort he gave.

She rode next to Lewis for a while and talked in a loud voice with Old Rivers about the eagle feathers for John. "Where can we find some?"

"They are everywhere if you are looking," he said. His voice was not loud, and she had to study his lips as he spoke to make out the words.

Nellie looked around. She saw no eagle feathers, just a dusty road churned by horses' hooves and people's feet and wagon wheels. Rocks jutted out at places, and deep grooves marked where heavy wagons had journeyed before them, both requiring Nellie to watch the road carefully so Midnight wouldn't stumble.

"Where?" She rode as close to Old Rivers's wagon as she thought was safe so she could better hear his words.

"Wherever the eagle soars. Where he looks for food in the river."

Nellie knew an eagle had thousands of feathers, so it was bound to lose a few most days, but the bird was not seen every day like the sparrow. Nor had she spotted any when they were camped near the Hiwassee. But the king of birds wouldn't want to fly around people.

"Around water?" she asked.

"Around big water," he said.

"Thanks." Nellie rode back up to John and told him they should look closely when they came to big water.

"We will cross the mighty Mississippi," he said.

"Then that's where we'll find them for sure, but we will cross the Tennessee River tomorrow," she said. "I heard Edoda talking with the others. We cross at Blythe's Ferry."

Now John's smile stretched wide. He nodded. "We will keep an eye open."

As the sun climbed, the day grew hotter, and the sun tortured both those walking and those riding. Etsi insisted Nellie put on a bonnet, and Nellie was glad of the shade for her eyes.

Nellie dropped back at least ten wagons to talk with Morning Sun, who rode in the wagon with her older brother and etsi. She climbed on Nellie's pony for a little while, and the girls rode back and forth between the Deerborns' wagon ahead of the Starr wagon and then back to Morning Sun's wagon, where the family slaves walked alongside. They helped Morning Sun climb back into the family wagon.

"We're going to cross the Tennessee before nightfall," Lewis told Nellie after hearing the news from other boys, who rode from the front of the wagon train to the back.

We are making good time today, Nellie thought. She rode along awhile longer, then slipped off Midnight to give him a rest. Besides, she felt guilty for riding when other people along the wagon train were walking. The white government provided wagons for those without, but they were limited to one wagon for every dozen or so people. Twelve people couldn't fit inside a wagon when it was reserved for belongings and provisions. Nellie figured half the people on the wagon train were walking. Elderly and young children walked alongside those in the prime of their years.

The creak of wagon wheels and the neighing of horses could not drown out the moan of the Cherokee who mourned this leaving of the homeland. As far as Nellie could see forward and as far as she could see on the road behind her were wagons and ponies and people walking along. The faces of the women looked as if they would never smile again.

Many others turned around like Nellie and looked back at the land they were leaving. They revered the land, these wooded hills and mountains, because of what was there before them. This land was a link with their ancestors. Nellie thought about the little grave of her dead infant sister. Etsi put flowers on the grave in the spring. They had left that grave behind. And the recent graves of her father's parents were left behind, too.

The wagon train came to a shallow creek, where water gurgled and bubbled over white stones. The crossing was slow. Nellie filled the water bucket with fresh water flowing above the crossing place that was muddied from so many horses crossing before them. Edoda let the oxen lower their heads to drink in the middle of the creek. Nellie's pony drank his fill, and then she climbed on his back, and they rode across the creek. It was Old Rivers's turn to let his team drink.

Old Rivers had recovered from his cold, and praise the Lord, he had not caught one of the many diseases that had claimed so many lives at the stockade. Most everyone on this wagon train was healthy. Some who had sick family members had left them in the care of others to await a later wagon train. But Nellie knew that some of them would not be making the journey to the new land. And the ones who had brought their sick ones with them, well, how could they survive riding in a wagon that jarred them with every turn of the wheels?

Bitterness crept into her heart. Bitterness against the white men who were forcing them to leave this beautiful land.

Nellie turned back and watched Old Rivers drive his team up the bank of the creek.

"Hee-yah!" he called to the oxen, and his wagon was out of the creek bed and the next in line quickly took his place.

This day of travel was just like the trip they had made when the soldiers had forced them from their homes back in June, except this was a much larger group than then. And the dust was thicker, and the sun was hotter.

"Nellie!" Etsi called from the wagon. "Here!"

Nellie stretched out her hand and took cornbread from her etsi. She had never eaten while riding Midnight. Eating a meal had been a ritual, a time of thanking God for the food, and a time of fellowship with her family. Now she whispered a prayer of thanks and greedily ate the cornbread while keeping her balance on her pony.

"Keep on going," a Light Horse said as he trotted his horse past the Starr wagon toward the front of the wagon train. He kept yelling encouragement to the people as he passed different wagons. Other members of the Cherokee police walked their horses on the edges of the long parade of walkers and wagons, keeping order.

At the stockade, they had tried to keep white alcohol merchants from peddling their whiskey to Cherokee men. Edoda said it was a hard job, since many a Cherokee brave had lost heart and thought he could find release and escape from the life of waiting in the heat through a bottle of whiskey. Now on the trail, a few Cherokee men dropped out of the line as the wagon train came upon a white trader with bottles to sell. He plied his trade out of a wagon stopped broadside next to the road, so that those coming toward it could see it from a long distance.

"A disgrace," Edoda said from his perch on the wagon seat, reins in hands, but he said it loud enough for Nellie to hear, and she figured he was saying it for her benefit.

She nodded her assurance. Of course, she would stay away from anyone who touched alcohol. Edoda had lectured her plenty of times about the harm alcohol could do. To show she understood, she dropped back, motioned for Lewis to follow her, and cut between their wagon and Old Rivers's wagon to ride on the side opposite the alcohol peddler.

"Edoda on the warpath again," Lewis said.

Nellie grinned at Lewis's little joke. How amazing it felt for her mouth to form a smile. On a day when her heart cried, it was wonderful to grab a bit of happiness. Not that she was happy to see the alcohol merchant, but it was good to hear Lewis's joke about Edoda.

"We have picked up some families from the first wagon train," Lewis said as he paced Blaze alongside Midnight. "Their wagons broke down—wheels, I think—and they are just now able to get back on the road."

"Where do you get all your information?" Nellie asked.

Lewis laughed. "I am all ears. And if I don't hear what Reverend Bushyhead tells the others, one of my friends hears it and tells me."

"Are we still crossing the Tennessee today?"

"We are making good time, but today is the first day, and everyone is strong."

"But getting more tired by the minute," Nellie said. She had mostly ridden, but she had walked awhile, and she couldn't imagine having to walk the entire way.

"We have also lost some members of this group," Lewis said. He took his hat off and slapped it against his thigh, wiped the sweat off his forehead with the back of his hand, and replaced his hat. "Some have run off when the Light Horse aren't nearby."

"Where are they going? What will they do?"

"I don't know. I guess they're going back in the mountains if they can hide from the whites."

The road was lined with woods now, and Lewis turned to stare through the trees. "I bet I can get a squirrel for supper."

"But there is to be food brought to the night camp, isn't there?"

"Supposed to be, but the people who joined our train say that so far it has been salt pork and salt pork and more salt pork. We might as well have something different to start the journey."

Lewis called to Edoda that he was going to hunt. "I'll use Smoke Cloud's blowgun!"

"Ask Smoke Cloud to go with you!" Edoda responded.

"I could do it alone," Lewis said, but only for Nellie to hear. Just the same, he dropped back a wagon and talked with Smoke

Cloud, who climbed from the wagon seat and fished his blowgun out of the back, all the while the wagon moved forward.

Lewis tied Blaze to the back of the wagon, and the two walked toward the woods. A Light Horse steered his horse toward them.

Nellie couldn't hear the conversation, but she watched as the policeman motioned them to go on.

An hour passed before Lewis and Smoke Cloud rejoined them, each carrying a skinned squirrel. Old Rivers stopped the wagon. Smoke Cloud plunged the squirrels in a pot that clanged against the side of the wagon. With the dipper of his water bucket, he added water, then he climbed back on board. Lewis jumped on Blaze.

"We had to go quite a ways into the woods," he said, "or we wouldn't have been so long."

The sun was in the western sky when Reverend Bushyhead called a halt to the first day's journey. The first wagon pulled off the road in a big pasture. Then the second one followed, went past it, and stopped. The next wagon went past both and stopped and so on until it was the Starrs' turn to stop for the night.

"You said we were crossing the Tennessee today," Nellie told Lewis.

He had resumed his traveling up and down the wagon train, and he had more news.

"Forward scouts say we are stalled at the ferry. It will take us awhile to cross, but we will begin at sunup. Reverend Bushyhead wants us to all be on one side of the river for the night, and if we started crossing now, we would have to split up. There is another wagon train ahead of us."

Reverend Bushyhead's helpers directed workers to dig a slit

trench for bathroom needs. Fires were lit for cooking, and Etsi cut up and fried the squirrels.

After the night meal, Reverend Bushyhead held a prayer service, where he thanked God for bringing them all safely through the first day of the journey. Not all the Cherokee attended the service. Some men were drunk and shouting out bad names for the white men who forced them to leave their land. From another part of the campground, Nellie heard the rhythmic sounds of drumbeats and of dancers shaking turtle rattles. Cherokee voices were lifted in echoing shaman chants.

But in her part of the camp, things were quieting down.

"Tonight we sleep under the wagon," Edoda said. "It's our new roof."

"Can I sleep under the stars?" Lewis asked.

"If you like," Edoda said.

Nellie liked lying on the ground and looking up at the stars, too. As the dancers finished their dance, quiet fell on the camp, and she heard the sound of a woman weeping—a sound that had been with them constantly throughout the day. She blocked it out and concentrated on the stars. They were the same stars she had seen just last night, miles away. And they were the same stars she would see in the new land. That thought comforted her, and she drifted off to sleep.

CHAPTER 8

John's Plan

Early the next morning after the first meal of the day, the wagons lined up, this time in the opposite order from when they started out. The Starr wagon was closer to the end of the long line than the front. As soon as they reached Blythe's Ferry, progress stopped. As a few wagons were taken across the river, the others waited, some impatiently.

Nellie was one of the more patient ones, for she saw this as the perfect opportunity to help John with his search for eagle feathers. With Etsi's permission, she and John rode their ponies along the river.

"I don't think eagles would be around the ferry. Too many people," Nellie said.

"My edoda said they could be around fast water. Eagles are the best fishermen. They go where the fish are."

"So we need the pools before rapids?"

"Yes. I wish we knew the river." He looked both upstream and downstream.

"Well, this has to be the narrow place or the ferry would be somewhere else."

"True. But how does that help us decide which way to go?"

"I think that way." Nellie pointed downstream. "I don't know why, except it could get faster. Or that way." She pointed upstream. "Maybe in the wider parts there are rocks that make white water."

"Just like I said, I wish we knew the river," John said.

"Well, we've got to go somewhere quick, or we'll run out of time. Etsi said we should cross before the sun is straight up."

"My edoda says it could take all day."

This arguing is getting us nowhere, Nellie decided. "You want to split up—me go upstream and you go down?"

"No, let's stay together." He clucked at his pony and started upstream. "If we don't find some in a mile or so, we can come back and go the other direction."

Nellie agreed with the simple plan and directed Midnight to follow John's pony. They followed an animal path that meandered beside the river. Nellie watched the ground for eagle feathers, but her watchfulness strayed to the tall trees that bordered the river, some with trunks so wide, it would take several men with their hands linked to form a circle around them. The cloudless blue sky held three big birds soaring on the warm air currents. But they were hawks, not eagles. A blue jay chattered on a low branch ahead of them and flew off when they came near.

"Eagles build nests in trees, not always in cliff alcoves," she said, giving information she had learned last night from Old Rivers.

John looked up as they passed under the heavy branches of a massive oak tree. "I don't think I could climb a tree like that. Too high."

"I wouldn't climb it either," Nellie said, "but there would likely be eagle feathers beneath a tree with a nest."

She looked out on the river and saw a tree limb floating by, moving oddly fast, for the smooth surface didn't hint at the currents in the depths of the water. This wonderful peaceful place was still on Cherokee land. Or it was once Cherokee land.

Not long ago, Cherokee land stretched even farther north, Edoda had told her. The white government had taken more and more land with their treaties and unfulfilled promises, but the one that forced her family on the wagon train was the ultimate false treaty. The Cherokee had adopted so many of the white man's ways. Their lives were nearly identical to those of the white settlers in many ways, except there was a deeper connection between the Cherokee and nature.

"This is our land," Nellie said aloud, although she didn't really mean to say it to John.

He cast a sly look at her.

"Why do you say that?"

"It's so beautiful. The river is deep and broad. The sky is blue and endless. A Cherokee wind brings a coolness to take away the heat of the sun. And now we are forced to leave this land. My heart is sad."

"We are not leaving," John said with a fierceness in his voice that she had never heard before.

"Of course, we're leaving. When our turn comes, we'll cross the river. Your wagon is three behind ours."

"Yes, but we are not going. My edoda says this is the time to make our escape. We will unload furniture from the wagon to make room for all of us inside. My grandmother, my aunt and uncle, and my cousins. And then we will drive to yonder hill before the Light Horse can stop us. They will be busy keeping order on the other side of the river."

"But the soldiers that rounded us up said—"

"Yes, rounded us up like cattle. Well, we are not going across the river." His eyes widened as if he realized he had said too much. "Nellie, you can't tell anybody. Promise?"

She hesitated. Was keeping this silent the same thing as lying, which she knew was wrong?

"Nellie! Promise?"

Edoda had once told her that she could be an example to others but not a controller of other people's lives. This must be an instance of that.

"We are going to the new land, even though we don't want to."

"And we are not. Promise, Nellie?"

"I will tell no one, but I think it is wrong." As soon as she said the words, she regretted them. That was being judgmental, and she knew that was not the way of a friend.

"Doesn't matter. My edoda has decided. Now, let's ride back the other way and see how many wagons have crossed. I don't see any signs of eagles up here."

They rode southwest along the river, with Nellie's mind full of John's secret. Would Edoda think she had done the right thing to promise silence?

At the ferry, the Starr wagon was nowhere near the front of the line. Edoda was standing by the oxen but was not on the wagon. She could easily go ask him what she should do, but wasn't that breaking her promise?

Instead, she waved and motioned that they were going farther downstream. Again, John's pony led the way, and she followed on Midnight.

"We may not find any feathers," Nellie said in a voice loud enough for John to hear. "Old Rivers said this is where eagles come in the winter, and it is not yet time. But there could be some early birds."

"Doesn't matter," John said. "We know there are golden eagles near our home. And even though the white men have taken our house, we will find a place to live where eagles soar."

"But how will you live?"

"My edoda says we will live by the old ways of his forefathers. We will hunt and fish, and we can clear land to plant."

"Where will you get seed?"

He shrugged. "From all around us. It is there for the taking, the drying, and the planting. And we brought some with us to use in the new land."

He held a low branch for her to pass under and waited for her to ride alongside him where the animal path was wider.

"Then this is a new plan? You meant to go all the way to the new land when we started yesterday?"

He sighed deeply, just as he had yesterday morning when their journey began. "The sorrow is too much," he said simply.

"It is for everyone," Nellie said. "Don't you want to be with your people?"

"Many of our family will go back with us. We will not be ordered off our ancient lands by intruders." His words sounded like those spoken by an older person, and Nellie figured he was quoting his edoda.

"Did you have a family council?"

"Last night. It is decided, Nellie. There is no turning back now."

The stubborn set of his jaw told Nellie that it was true. She could not influence him to change his family's mind.

"Then I hope you find peace."

They rode along in silence, the Cherokee way. Speak little and listen big, Edoda always said. But John wasn't talking, either.

No eagle feathers could be found along the river. No nests sat high in the trees. But Nellie's thoughts were not on eagles. She was losing a good friend. She would never see John again after this day.

The bitterness she felt against the white men who had forced them on this march intensified. She tried to rid her heart of hatred, but instead her heart felt heavy and angry.

"Let's go back," John said. "It's no use to look further."

They rode back to the ferry in silence. What was left to say?

The supply wagons were being transported across the water, and the Starr wagon had been pushed farther back in line, Edoda told them when they arrived back at the wagon train.

Light Horse patrols still directed the transfer to the other bank. Nellie could see some of the Cherokee policemen on the other side of the river.

She rode back to the Deerborn wagon with John. Several family members had unloaded some furniture.

"We need to repack," John's edoda said in a loud voice, loud enough for the Light Horse nearby to hear. "We will make room for someone else to ride."

"Is the plan going forward?" John whispered to his edoda when the Light Horse moved on.

"Yes. As soon as they move a few more wagons, there will only be one or two Light Horse left."

"I'll be back," Nellie said. She rode to the Starr wagon to see if Etsi needed anything. She had been out gathering mullein and lamb's quarter to put with her healing herbs.

"It could be another hour before we can cross," Etsi said.

Nellie looked across the river. The last wagon to leave the ferry was headed up the bank incline. It would join the others as they moved on down the road a few miles before nightfall. So each ferry load had to catch up with the train. That would space out the long line of Cherokee on the trail. And it would be much later after they made camp when their leader, Reverend Bushyhead, found out that the Deerborn wagon wasn't with them.

To pass a little time, Nellie tied Midnight to the wagon and sat on the tailgate with her writing supplies. She wrote about the first day of the journey. She did not mention John's plan. What if it didn't happen? What if the Light Horse made them stay in line?

"Nellie."

She looked up from her writing paper. John sat on his horse beside the Starr wagon.

"It is time. The Light Horse have been called across the river."

Nellie looked toward the ferry. The last of the mounted Cherokee police were nearly to the other side.

"We will wait until the ferry is back here and is loading. I just wanted to tell you good-bye."

"May God be with you," Nellie said.

"And with you," John said.

He turned his horse back to his wagon. Nellie put away her writing materials and climbed on Midnight. She rode from the line of wagons to a small rise so she could see the Deerborn wagon clearly.

She expected a dramatic scene—a cry to the oxen from John's edoda and a race to the hills where the family would disappear. Instead, the Deerborn wagon moved quietly out of line and went toward the river but veered north as if they were looking over the area for something. The last Nellie saw of the wagon, it was following the curve of the river. John lifted his hand, not in a big wave, but in a quiet gesture of farewell. Nellie held her hand to her heart. So this was a final good-bye to a lifelong friend she had thought she might one day marry.

"Good-bye, John," she whispered and held her hand up toward the sky. For a brief moment she felt defiance toward the white men, and she was proud John would remain on Cherokee land.

She turned Midnight and rode to the Starr wagon. When it was their turn, she urged her pony onto the ferry. Edoda had already driven the team onboard the flat wooden surface.

As the ferry moved slowly across the Tennessee River, Nellie stood beside Midnight and stared into the muddy water. She wished she could see the future. She wished she could see where John's family would go. She wished them peace and happiness. But could there be happiness for any of them?

She looked back at the line of wagons awaiting their turn. Then she turned to watch the landing of the ferry and led Midnight off the ramp onto the other shore.

CHAPTER 9

The Trail Westward

On the west side of the Tennessee River, Nellie's heart sank like a stone in the water. She didn't know if she was now off ancient Cherokee earth, but it felt like it. It felt like she had crossed into the unknown.

She rode Midnight beside the wagon.

"Etsi, do you need something, anything?"

"Do not worry, Nellie. I am fine."

Her etsi was not yet large with child, but Nellie could tell through Etsi's dress that the baby was growing. In less than four months, she would have a new brother or sister. In less than four months, they would be in the new land.

She'd heard the men talk about the trip. It should take less than three months if everything went well. If they made the miles every day that they made yesterday, they could easily do that. A journey of eight hundred miles could be broken down to walking ten miles a day, and they had made more than that yesterday. It was three miles from home to the mission school, and it took her about an hour when she walked, much less time on Midnight.

By doing simple arithmetic, she worked it out to less than four hours a day of movement should put them ten miles farther down the trail toward the new Cherokee land. Of course, the old ones could not move as fast as she, and there seemed to be a large number of old ones walking, carrying heavy burdens. But they had traveled much longer than four hours yesterday. And she was sure they would do the same most days.

They had been delayed enormously today with the ferry crossing. Waiting hours to move forward took its toll on the mind. But that was over. They were moving forward now, trying to catch the wagons that had crossed the river before them.

Yes, even with delays like this one, and even if they didn't travel on Sunday as Reverend Bushyhead told them last night, they would still be in the new Cherokee country before the baby was born.

Nellie rode past the Starr wagon just to see what was ahead. The land varied when the road passed through forests and when it passed through cleared land. She saw few houses along the road and, so far, no real towns. There were hills, though, and the oxen and horses slowed down as they pulled the heavily laden wagons.

She passed more walkers than she did wagons. Not for the first time in her life did she realize how fortunate she was to have a pony. Edoda had commented many times about the differences in the poor and the wealthy, and how there were not many Cherokee in between the two extremes. It was the same with the white men, he said, and although the Starrs had the new house and the store, he said their family was not really in the wealthy class. They were part of the few families in the upper middle. He said he sometimes felt bad that the store was doing well. It made him feel more white than Cherokee.

He believed the Cherokee thought more of living and the white men thought more of getting. Yet the Starr family lived very well and had gotten very much. They worked hard, but they enjoyed play, too. Many times, Edoda had said that real wealth was in things that feed the spirit. Beautiful things. Things that brought joy like a field of daisies dancing in the wind or the music of a stream gurgling over stones.

Ahead, Nellie spotted Morning Sun. Her friend, family members, and their slaves were walking alongside the wagon to lighten the load as the oxen strained to make the hill. Nellie got off Midnight and walked beside her friend.

"This journey is taking a long time. Are we there yet?" Morning Sun asked with a laugh.

Nellie laughed, too. It was an odd sound to her ears. She had not laughed much lately, and it felt good.

She could see how Morning Sun got her name. She was joyful like the morning sun. Oh, sometimes she could be like the sun on cloudy days, but more often she was bright and happy and smiling.

"I think we have a few more days on the trail," Nellie said. "We should make it in less than three months."

"That *is* a long time," Morning Sun said.

"Yes, but there is nothing we can do about it except go forward," Nellie said, echoing something Old Rivers had said.

"One foot in front of the other and switch and switch and switch," Morning Sun said in a singsong voice. Morning Sun linked arms with Nellie, and they walked, skipped, and danced forward. They didn't dance in a spiral like the stars overhead, in the traditional Cherokee way of dancing, but they danced forward.

"You girls are silly," Morning Sun's brother said as he plodded up the steep hill.

Although breathless from climbing the road, Morning Sun said, "We are going forward. Like it or not, that's what we're doing. So we might as well enjoy doing it."

Her attitude matched the attitude of Old Rivers, and Nellie liked that. Too many times lately, she had asked what crime the Cherokee had committed to be thrown off their land. There was no answer to that question, but there was no use fighting what had happened.

"One foot in front of the other," Nellie sang with Morning Sun. Her heart was lightened, and it had been so heavy after John's family left. Nellie walked with Morning Sun until they crested the long hill and Morning Sun could ride on the wagon.

On the ride back to the Starr wagon, Nellie looked around for joyful things to feed her spirit. She heard an owl in the woods calling *whoo*.

"Why are you not asleep?" Nellie called to the owl. He answered with another *whoo*.

Blue flowers bloomed on the bank of a ditch. She wanted to pick one for her etsi, but with no vase to put it in, no table to set it on to brighten a room, she did not. She wouldn't harm a flower for a moment's joy, just to watch it wilt and die.

She rode beside the wagon until they reached the long hill. Then she insisted that Etsi ride Midnight. Nellie walked alongside Sarah, while Edoda drove the team. Their wagon was so full that it was a laborious pull for the oxen.

Once they crested the top and Etsi and Sarah climbed on board for the ride downhill, Edoda said, "We may have to double team with Old Rivers to make the next hill."

And that's exactly what they had to do. With both teams of oxen hitched to the Starr wagon, it was still a hard pull. Then Edoda unhitched the oxen and drove the two teams downhill to hitch them to Old Rivers's wagon.

Nellie, Sarah, and Etsi sat on the ground in the shade of the wagon.

"At this rate, it will take us forever to get to the new land," Nellie said.

"I have heard that Missouri does not have the glorious mountains of Tennessee," Etsi said. "It is flatter, and it will be easier travel."

"Glorious mountains," Sarah said slowly, as if the phrase rolled deliciously off her tongue.

Etsi smiled for a brief moment. "They are glorious mountains, and I will miss them," she said, and then she cried.

Sarah cried with her, and Nellie couldn't hold back her tears. What a day of conflicting emotions. One moment she was dancing on the road with Morning Sun, and the next she was crying at the side of the road beside a stalled wagon. She'd felt defiance toward the white men when John's family rode away, and now she felt bitterness toward them because they were taking the glorious mountains from her people. She knew both feelings were wrong. She should turn the other cheek, as she had learned from the Bible. She should forgive those who trespassed against her, but her heart and mind warred in turmoil, and she was incapable of forgiveness.

They were still wiping tears when another double-teamed wagon grunted to the top of the hill. Those folks unhitched, and a man drove the teams downhill to get another wagon. At least a dozen women and children traveled with the other wagon, and Nellie struck up a conversation with them. When Sarah repeated the phrase "glorious mountains," the entire bunch wept.

Edoda, Old Rivers, Smoke Cloud, and Lewis made it to the top of the hill.

"What's this?" Edoda asked.

"We've lost our glorious mountains," Nellie said.

"But we have not lost each other," Edoda said. "We have much to be thankful for, so let's not dwell on what we have lost."

He helped Etsi and Sarah onto the wagon, and the wagon rumbled downhill. Nellie followed on Midnight.

Of course Edoda was right. Of course. On the long road the rest of that day, Nellie repeated in her mind that they had a lot to be thankful for. She asked God to help her see the happy side of life.

That evening, the sunset was spectacular as clouds had moved in, and half the sky glowed with pinks and purples. But the clouds moved on without dropping one speck of rain. And after the sun's colorful display disappeared, the evening seemed gray, and Nellie again felt dispirited.

After the evening prayer service led by Reverend Bushyhead, Edoda stayed at the gathering spot to talk with him. The rest of the family walked back to their wagon. It was too hot to go right to sleep, so Nellie sat leaning against a wagon wheel.

Old Rivers sat down beside her.

"Did you find any eagle feathers today?" he asked.

"No."

"Did you look hard?"

"We looked very hard. We rode up and down the river, but there was not one sign of eagles."

"I found a feather." He had been holding his left hand to his side, and he held it out to her—a golden eagle feather. "You may give this to your friend."

"Thank you." She took the feather. "But I can't give it to him."

She didn't want to say more. She had promised. But weren't John and his family now beyond the long reach of the Light Horse? She couldn't imagine some of the Cherokee policemen leaving their responsibilities to the wagon train to trail after the Deerborn family.

Edoda came back to the wagon and squatted in front of Nellie.

"Do you know anything about the Deerborn family?" he asked. "Reverend Bushyhead says the evening report shows their wagon is missing. Should we send out a search party to help them?"

"I do not believe they need help," Nellie said.

"What do you know, Nellie?" Edoda asked softly.

"I have given my promise not to say anything. Wouldn't it be wrong to break that promise?"

"There have been deserters on other wagon trains," Edoda said. "And there will be more on the trains behind us. Some people do not think they can live away from our homelands. But they are wrong. We must," he said. "We must."

Old Rivers spoke up. "Many people fear the unknown, but we must face our fears and go forward. All of us. The Deerborn family faces the unknown going away from the trail, as we do who go along the trail."

"I do not believe we should send out a search party," Nellie said. Saying that didn't violate her promise, did it?

She handed the feather back to Old Rivers.

"Keep it," he said. "It will remind you of your friend. He is gone, but you have memories that will always be with you."

"Thank you," Nellie said. She would keep the feather with her writing materials, and each time she saw it, she would say a little prayer that John and his family were finding their way, although it was down a different path than the one she was traveling.

"I must tell Jesse Bushyhead," Edoda said. "Good night, Nellie."

"I cannot tell—"

"You did not tell me anything I didn't already know," he said. "You kept your promise. But sometimes it is best not to make a promise."

After Edoda left to find their leader, Nellie made her pallet on the ground so she could again watch the stars. How much had happened since she looked up at these same stars last night. John was somewhere back in the old land, never to be seen again. But John could be looking up at the same stars as she. So they were not that far apart, were they?

When she looked at the stars tomorrow night, where would they be and what would have changed by then? If only she could see the future, she could be sure that things would be fine in the new land. Old Rivers said they must face their fears, and she guessed she would have to do that.

A voice in her head, her own voice, told her that she was not alone facing the future. God was with her wherever she went. She took peace from the thought and went to sleep.

The next morning, the routine was the same as the day before. Women fixed breakfast. Men hitched the livestock to the wagons. Children carried water buckets to wagons. The slit ditches were covered, and they were off for another day of riding and walking in the ceaseless sun.

The third day of the journey turned into the fourth and the fifth and the sixth. The only thing that distinguished one day from the next was the availability of supplies. On the sixth day, the food supply merchant had only moldy crackers to disperse. Quickly, the routine was set to cook at communal fires. The order came to use firewood cautiously as more wagon trains were coming behind them.

Already there was less game to be found along the trail. Those who had passed this way before them had sent rabbits and squirrels and deer scampering to safer areas. Lewis and Smoke Cloud rode farther and farther from the train in search of game for supper. Their skill with blowguns saved them from eating the same fare as the rest of the wagon train. Salt pork and cornbread every meal. Of course, now there were moldy crackers, too.

On the seventh day—Sunday—they rested. Reverend Bushyhead said they would not travel on the Sabbath. Exhausted, the old and young alike lay around the large camp, rubbing sore muscles and taking cat naps, trying to restore lagging energy.

Nellie and her family attended the Sunday morning service and sang hymns in the Cherokee language, just as they had with the evening services.

"A week we've been on the trail," Edoda said while the family ate supper that evening. Salt pork and cornbread, again.

"There are many sick ones," Old Rivers said. "We will make room in the wagon to carry the sick."

They piled some of Old Rivers's belongings in the crowded Starr wagon and made room for an old woman, She-Who-Sings, and a young boy, not three years old, and his mother to ride in the back.

The next morning, they began the journey again.

CHAPTER 10

The Illness Strikes

"I am plenty old enough to nurse," Nellie said. Etsi had wanted to nurse She-Who-Sings in Old Rivers's wagon, but Nellie and Edoda put up a fuss. Nellie did not want Etsi around any sickness. If she caught the sickness, the baby might be harmed.

As the dry dusty days rolled by, the Cherokee walkers grew more exhausted. Putting one foot in front of the other was an effort, and Reverend Bushyhead called for several rest stops during each day.

Each time the wagons stopped, Nellie would climb into Old Rivers's wagon and force She-Who-Sings to take an herbal drink. She bathed the old woman's face and hands in water that grew warm as the sun rose high in the sky. The boy coughed the deep hack of whooping cough, and his young mother bent over him, holding him close to her heart.

As the days passed, Nellie watched the old woman grow weak and thin. She should have known She-Who-Sings would not get better, but she was unprepared when she was bathing her and the woman's breathing changed. Long gaps of time passed between breaths. Her breathing slowed and slowed and slowed, until Nellie heard a rattle in her throat. She-Who-Sings drew one final breath. Then nothing.

Nellie screamed.

She didn't realize she was still screaming when Old Rivers

pulled her out of the wagon. Etsi rushed to her side and held her tight.

"It is hard, I know," she crooned. "But it was time for She-Who-Sings to cross to the other side."

Edoda rode Midnight to tell Revered Bushyhead what had happened. Old Rivers covered the body with a blanket. The wagon train continued on until it reached the evening campgrounds near a spring.

Several men took turns digging the grave, while others built a rough coffin from young saplings. The old woman's body was wrapped in the covering blanket and placed in the casket.

"We can't just leave her alongside the road," Nellie said through her tears. She sat on the ground beside the wagon.

"We will give her a proper burial, but that is all we can do," Edoda said.

"I will make her a marker," Lewis said. He patted Nellie on the shoulder. "I imagine she is singing a pretty tune in heaven now. She never was much of a singer here on earth."

"Lewis!" Nellie gasped. "That is speaking unkindly of the dead."

"That is speaking the truth," Lewis said.

"Lewis is right," Old Rivers said. "She-Who-Sings always had a melody in her heart, but it didn't come out of her mouth in a pleasant way. Still, her songs were joyful."

"We should celebrate that she has finally found a real voice," Lewis said.

Nellie shook her head, but her cheeks were dried of tears, and she felt better. Certainly She-Who-Sings was better off. She was a Christian woman who was ready to meet her Maker, and she was no longer trapped in a sick, old body in a hard, jarring wagon.

"Do you think an angel gave her a harp?" Nellie asked.

"Made of pure gold," Lewis said.

Nellie smiled. She had not known the old woman until this wagon train. But she had grown attached to her, and she would miss her.

That evening, Reverend Bushyhead led the funeral service. When it was time to sing the hymns, Nellie sang her sweetest and strongest in honor of She-Who-Sings. Some men shoveled dirt on top of the coffin.

In other places in the camp, shamans danced around campfires and threw powder into the flames to ward off evil spirits of illness.

Nellie prayed the other Cherokee who believed in the shaman's magic would believe in the one true God, who was surely listening to the songs of She-Who-Sings.

The next morning, Lewis placed a cross made of two strong twigs bound with ivy in the brown dirt atop the grave. Nellie stood beside him, whispered a prayer, and wiped tears. Then she climbed on Midnight and rode alongside the Starr wagon as the wagon train moved on down the trail. She did not look back.

Two weeks had passed since Nellie had first nursed She-Who-Sings. She felt as if two months had passed, instead. She had not seen Morning Sun during that time, except briefly at the evening services and at the funeral, and now she sought the comfort of her friend.

The two girls walked side-by-side down the dusty road. On this day, they were solemn as Nellie told Morning Sun about watching She-Who-Sings die.

"Were you scared?" Morning Sun asked.

"Yes, and I am ashamed that I screamed."

"You should not be ashamed of that. The next time, you won't scream."

"I pray there is no next time," Nellie said.

"There are so many sick. My etsi says it's amazing that there has not been a death before now."

Nellie nodded in agreement. "I know. But this is hard."

"It is good for She-Who-Sings and hard for you."

"You are right. We should celebrate for her."

"And we should sing," Morning Sun said. She linked arms with Nellie and sang, "One foot in front of the other and switch and switch and switch."

Nellie raised her voice in song, but she felt much older than the girl she had been weeks earlier when they had first made up the song and danced down the dusty road.

That night, Nellie looked up at a dark sky. No twinkling silver stars. For several weeks, she had gazed at the same stars in the same sky. But tonight clouds blocked the stars and the moon. The night was solid black. Nellie awakened early the next morning. The birds weren't singing, but she could hear the wind blow the branches of trees.

The sky growled as the Cherokee broke camp. The normal chores were done and the wagons had begun moving forward when the wind drew strength and howled.

A few moments later, the first drops of rain touched her face, her arms, and her legs, clamped against Midnight's lean sides.

"Rain!" Lewis shouted from his position beside Old Rivers's wagon.

"Rain!" Nellie echoed.

"Want in the wagon?" Old Rivers called.

"No!" Nellie wanted to shout and dance. Thunder boomed. And where she normally shied away from the sound, she reveled in it. Jagged lightning crackled overhead, but she did not cringe from the sight. Rain poured from the sky as if She-Who-Sings was dumping buckets from heaven.

"The drought is broken!" Edoda shouted above the sound of the furious storm. "Praise the Lord, the drought is broken!"

It felt that way to Nellie, too, and to other Cherokee who stomped in the deep ruts that had turned to puddles of water. She splashed and laughed and put her head back for the rain to hit her eyes, her cheeks, her chin. She opened her mouth and let the rainwater quench a deep thirst she didn't know she had.

Etsi hung every pot they had off the sides of the wagon to catch the rain. With the springs being low from the drought, water had been very dear, and its use limited to drinking and cooking.

"We're washing clothes tonight!" she called to Nellie.

How wonderful it would be to wear clean clothes. At the first part of the journey, they had changed every couple days, but that quickly ended. Nellie had been in the same yellow cotton dress for a week now. With the days repeating the same heat, the miles that seemed like the same as the ones before, and the same chores, she had done as the others on the wagon train and just laid down on a blanket to sleep, then gotten up and started the next day.

Last year at this time, she would never have dreamed she would be wearing the same dress for a week. Mending clothes, which used to be one of her chores, was a thing of the past. Her dress was torn where it had caught on nails inside the wagon when she was nursing She-Who-Sings. She had spilled broth on it, too, but it didn't matter.

The rain kept up most of the day, but the wagons kept rolling forward. The walkers, who were used to wiping sweat off their foreheads, now wiped off cool water.

That night, Nellie helped Etsi with the laundry. They hung clothes on makeshift clothes lines and gathered them in the next morning, even though they had not completely dried in the air, humid from the rain. Etsi spread them over the furniture in the wagon for them to dry.

The heat of summer disappeared with the rain, and the air turned chilly. The next night, Nellie curled up in her blanket, and when daybreak came, she didn't want to turn out of her cozy cocoon to face the day.

What before was a dusty rutted road had now turned into a mud pit. Even on Midnight, Nellie did not escape the mud bath the walkers endured. Wagon wheels threw mud up behind the wagons, and that was when they were turning well. Mud sucked the wheels deeper and deeper. Once, Edoda had to double-team the wagon to pull it out of a deep, muddy rut. Their wagon was not the only one to get stuck and have to be pulled out. Until autumn's brisk winds dried the mud into deeper ruts, the wagon train made a dismal three miles a day, and those few miles seemed to take forever.

Autumn had come, and with it came rains. Where before, Nellie had wanted relief from the heat and dryness, now she wanted the rains that came every three or four days to stop. Especially did she hate the rain at night. They slept under the wagon to stay out of the weather, but it still blew in on stormy nights, and her blanket was wet and her clothes were wet and her hair was wet. She was chilled to the bone.

The deep sound of whooping cough came from everywhere. The young boy who rode in Old Rivers's wagon got well. But others were sick with it, the very young and the very old especially.

The first frost came mid-October, and with it, the leaves magically changed from green to gold and scarlet and glowing orange. Nellie tried to feed her spirit with nature's show of colors, but other thoughts pushed her joy aside.

"I have always liked autumn," she told Old Rivers, who sat beside her near the campfire one night after the worship service. Many Cherokee huddled near the warmth of the flames, and as before, there were only a few campfires allowed to save firewood. "I like the brilliant colors of leaves, but now I think of them as the colors of death. No sooner do the leaves change colors than they fall off. Dead."

"It is the way of all things," Old Rivers said. "Everything has its season, just as the Bible says."

"But it is so sad," Nellie said.

"It is the way of all things," he repeated. "It is better you accept the ways of nature than fight them."

"Nellie."

She looked up when she heard her name to see Etsi holding the sleeping blankets. Quickly Nellie stood and took one end of a blanket and held it toward the fire. As soon as it warmed, Nellie rushed it to Sarah, so she could start the night with a warm blanket. They continued to hold blankets to the fire until all were heated, and the family bedded down under the wagon. This night they were camped in a large field of thick grass. Nellie thought the ground was like a straw tick mattress, maybe even softer. The night before, they had been on hard rocky soil.

Reverend Bushyhead had complained that a farmer had charged them for camping on his land, but Nellie thought the cost was worth it as she drifted off to sleep.

In the morning, the cost of sleeping on a soft bed of grass went way up. The Starrs' oxen as well as others' livestock had gorged themselves on poisonous plants and were sick. The animals were moved to another area and tended by their owners. The wagon train was stranded until the animals either got well or were replaced.

One of Edoda's oxen died. The other suffered mightily but regained strength. Old Rivers's oxen were staked well away from the poisonous plants, but Jesse Bushyhead said no one was going on until all were ready to travel.

While they waited for the oxen to recover, their wagon train was passed by a three-mile-long train on which Reverend Evan Jones was serving as a leader. Nellie watched the Cherokee pass by and saw that the faces of the travelers were as dispirited as the ones in her group.

The delay caused by slow travel on rainy days and the sick animals made Nellie think once more of her plan to be in the new land by the time Etsi's baby was born.

Etsi was looking thin, even though her belly was getting bigger. Nellie feared she was not eating enough, and sometimes she said she was not hungry and gave her meager share of salt pork and cornbread to her etsi.

Edoda was able to buy an ox from a nearby farmer, but the price was more than the ox was worth in the old days. That's how

Nellie was now thinking of the days before the journey. The old days. As if she were an old-timer now at twelve years old.

"We can't compare now to then," Edoda said, even as he complained about the price of the ox, which wasn't an equal physical match to his first one. "We are blessed that we have the money to buy one. I should not be so loud in crying foul."

Nellie thought he should shout it. He was being cheated by a white farmer. Once again the white man was taking advantage of them.

Finally, the journey began again.

But the outrages against the Cherokee continued. A ferry demanded an unheard of amount as a crossing fee. Sometimes supplies were late, and when that happened, the large group went hungry. Lewis and Smoke Cloud continued to hunt game, but many times, they came back empty-handed.

When supplies were early, Reverend Bushyhead asked folks to leave some of their belongings behind to make room for the extra supplies. He explained before the nightly prayer meeting that it took twelve wagons to carry enough food for three days for the people and the livestock. If suppliers met them early, there had to be a place to carry the supplies.

Lewis helped Edoda unload Nellie's trunk. He sold it for a fraction of its cost to a white man, but Nellie kept the clothes she had packed inside. They took up less space if they were just wadded up and stashed between other items. She could wash and iron them when they arrived at the new land. Even with extra food stuffs stacked at the far end of the wagon, Nellie kept her writing tools handy. She had been too tired to write the last week, but she intended to get back to her journal very soon.

CHAPTER 11

A Dark Heart

"Midnight!" Nellie screamed. She and Lewis had run from one end of the campground to the other this cold morning, but Midnight was gone.

"Did you stake her good?" Lewis asked for the tenth time.

"Of course. And even if she had pulled up the stake, she would not have wandered off. Someone stole her!"

They reported back to the Starr wagon. Edoda had already hitched the oxen to the wagon, and Etsi and Sarah sat on the seat. Camp was breaking up, and wagons and walkers were falling into line.

"Anything?" Nellie asked, tears blurring her vision.

"Your edoda will be right back," Etsi said. "He was looking—"

"I'm back," Edoda said, coming around the wagon from the other side. "I found nothing. She's gone."

"Who could have taken her—except the white men, of course?" Nellie felt like screaming at the top of her lungs that she hated the white men. Who else could have taken her pony but someone living near where they'd camped? The white men had already taken their homeland. Why not take a girl's pony?

Old Rivers came up behind her. "I don't have proof of this, but I think I know what happened."

Nellie whirled. "Did you find Midnight?"

"No. She's gone. But I believe she was traded for liquor."

"What? Who?" Nellie couldn't make sense of what he said.

"Someone said that Running Deer gave Midnight as payment for bottles of alcohol."

"Who said? Who did he give her to?"

"No one I can name. People are afraid of Running Deer when he has been drinking."

"Old Rivers, where is Midnight?" Nellie asked.

Old Rivers was climbing onto his wagon. "I don't know, but I suspect she is many miles down the road." He pointed the opposite direction the wagons were heading. "She will soon be traded for something else. Do you want to ride with us?"

"No. I'll walk," Nellie said. She stomped alongside the Starr wagon, her anger growing with every step. She wiped tears as the realization of her loss sank deeper into her heart.

She told Etsi she was going ahead to talk with Morning Sun, but it was not as easy on foot as it had been on Midnight.

It took a long time to reach Morning Sun's wagon. She was walking beside it, since the oxen were pulling it up another hill.

Nellie explained about Midnight's disappearance—how she hadn't heard a thing in the night, not a single neigh had awakened her. But this morning the pony was gone. She told what Old Rivers had heard about the trade.

"How horrible," Morning Sun said. "What can you do?" She coughed, as if the words had irritated her throat.

"Nothing." Nellie covered her face with her hands. Her dear pony, gone. Just like that.

Morning Sun put her arm around Nellie. "It'll be all right. You can get a new pony in the new land." Again, she coughed.

"It won't be the same."

"No, it won't be the same. Nothing will be the same."

They walked on while Nellie cried, and Morning Sun cried with her. Finally, Nellie dried her tears.

"I just want to go home," Nellie said.

"But you can't."

"I guess home now is a wagon."

"I guess home is where your friends and family are," Morning Sun said. This time she bent over with a cough that sounded deeper than before.

"Are you sick?" Nellie asked.

"I'm okay," Morning Sun said. "Just a cold."

The cough didn't sound like the deep whoop and wheeze of whooping cough, and Nellie had heard that enough to know the sound, so she was reassured by Morning Sun's words.

They crested the hill, where woods bordered both sides of the road. Nellie decided to sit in the warmth of the sun on a downed log and wait for her wagon. No sense in walking downhill to meet it and then climbing back up.

Nellie watched the Cherokee plod by. They had been on the move for nearly two months, and the endless journey and time and weather had taken their toll on her people. The faces she saw were shadows of their former selves. The old seemed older, more lines on their faces, deeper frowns on their lips. They no longer held their proud heads aloft. They wore downcast, dejected looks.

The funeral for She-Who-Sings had been the first in a long line of funerals. There had been days when they had buried more than one body along the trail.

Sickness was everywhere. Nellie had been so upset about Midnight's disappearance that she had shirked her duty as nurse to the sick man carried in Old Rivers's wagon. Well, with two children in there now along with their mothers who would not leave their sides, that man would get looked after. Still, it was her job.

There was a break in the parade of tired and sick people passing by. Probably a wagon broken, holding up the rest. The others would get it to the side of the road, and then they would pass by, always walking west.

They had passed Nashville recently. There had been more supplies there, and some of the barefoot Cherokee received shoes. There were more blankets, too. And they needed them for protection against the frigid days. Some mornings, they had crossed creeks with ice along the banks where the flowing water slowed.

And tents. The Starrs had received a tent, which did not do much to keep out the cold. But it helped to keep out the rain. Two days earlier, they had awakened to a thin blanket of snow on the tent and on the ground.

"An early winter," Old Rivers had said.

Just what they needed. Nellie sighed. She had railed against the harsh sun of September before the drought had broken, and now she sought the warmth of the sun as October turned to November.

The parade started in front of her again. More sad people. Sad like her. Finally, the Starr wagon topped the hill. Etsi was walking with Sarah, and she looked older, more tired than Nellie had ever seen her. As soon as Etsi saw Nellie, her expression changed. Not exactly a smile lit her face, but something like encouragement shone from her eyes.

That was what they were all doing. Putting up a better front to encourage each other. No, not all. Many of the Cherokee were so despondent, their eyes did not light up at anything.

Old Rivers's wagon crested the hill, and he waved to Nellie that he wanted to talk to her. He stopped the wagon, and she climbed on. Smoke Cloud was walking beside the wagon, and he continued walking.

"Hee-yah!" Old Rivers called to the team, and they started downhill, with the old man carefully holding on to the brake.

Nellie waited for him to say something. The silence bothered her, and she wondered if she were getting more like the white men who rushed to fill silence instead of letting it settle around them.

"You looked very sad sitting on the side of the road," Old Rivers finally said. "You are allowing your emotions to take your inner peace."

It was Nellie's turn to be silent. Yes, her emotions were in turmoil. She didn't know if she could identify them all. Anger at losing Midnight. No, she was distraught at losing Midnight. She'd had the pony for three years, and Midnight had become her best friend. She could talk to Midnight, and Midnight listened. Extreme sadness was mixed in with her feelings. And hatred was mixed in there, too.

What was missing was joy, happiness, and her inner peace.

"How do you capture the peace again?" Nellie asked.

"There are many ways," he said. "God gives us time, which heals our wounds. And you must drive out fear."

"Fear?" She had not thought that she was afraid. She trusted Edoda and Etsi to take care of her.

"Fear of the unknown. Fear of arriving at our new land and not finding it the place we had hoped for. Fear for your etsi and her baby. Fear is the destroyer of the human spirit. Ask God to help you let go of the bad voices of fear and hate in your mind, the bad thoughts that say how bad things are, and let peace settle in again."

"I want peace," Nellie said.

"Peace comes when we ask for it, not when we search for it. You need stillness and serenity, which is hard to find here." Old Rivers waved his hand at the long line of travelers ahead of them. "A woodland path is good medicine for a weary soul. The aged timber speaks to us."

They traveled in silence for a while. The road leveled out, and the wagons settled to a slow crawl. They crossed a shallow creek, and once they reached the other side, Old Rivers stopped his wagon.

"There is a path." He pointed to an animal trail. "Walk a bit among the aged timbers, and then come back to the wagons. You will find peace."

Nellie climbed down from the wagon and started down the path that bordered the creek. Tall trees crowded the narrow trail. Many had already lost their leaves, and when she looked up, she saw their winter silhouettes pressed against the blue sky.

Ahead was a downed tree, an aged timber whose time had come. This tree had gone through many changes in its long life. It had cycled through many seasons. Nellie studied the massive trunk. Growth circles told the life of the tree—wide circles for good years and narrow circles for bad years.

This is a narrow circle year for me, Nellie thought. Or was it a wide circle? Maybe her circles didn't just measure physical growth, like the lengthening of a bone, but maybe they measured the growth of her mind and her heart.

She was not the same person she had been before the white men took their land. She was not even the same person she had been when they had begun this journey. Her heart was hardened. Her joy at living had seeped away. What had been light was now heavy. She felt her heart was turning dark. She did not want a dark heart. She bowed her head and closed her eyes.

"Dear God, help me," she said in the silence of the woods. "Please help me find inner peace again. Please help me see the world in a different way—in a way that is full of the joy of daily living. Feed my spirit with nature's delights."

She opened her eyes and saw a mouse skitter across the dead leaves on the trail ahead of her. She heard a jaybird's shrill caw. On the north side of the downed log grew deep green moss. She bent down and examined it. A bug crawled along the bark and disappeared in a hole. The creek gurgled nearby.

There was life all around her, even on this cold day. Life went on—without Midnight, without She-Who-Sings, without an ancient homeland. And Nellie knew she could be bitter or she could be accepting and go on with her life. It was her choice.

She did not want a dark heart. She would not let her emotions take her inner peace.

With this resolve inside her, she retraced her steps to the road and hurried along to catch up with Old Rivers's wagon.

When he saw her, he stopped and climbed down. Smoke Cloud drove the team forward, and Old Rivers walked alongside Nellie.

"Your spirit is lighter," he said.

"I do not want a dark heart," Nellie said.

"You do not have a dark heart," he said. "Your heart is as red as a ripe apple in the sunlight. But sometimes an apple gets bruised when it falls from the tree. Or sometimes a worm eats its way inside. And then there are dark spots on the red apple. We must guard against spots on our hearts."

"Let go of the bad thoughts of fear and hatred in my mind, and let peace settle in," Nellie recalled his earlier words. "And I won't have dark spots on my heart."

"Yes. You are a smart girl and a very brave one," he said. "But you must be on guard against the bad voices, for they tend to return at hard times. Little by little, we get stronger. Little steps take us on a long journey." He motioned for Smoke Cloud to stop. He climbed on. "Want to ride?"

"I'll catch up with my family and walk," Nellie said. "And I'll check on the sick man at every rest stop."

Etsi and Sarah were riding again. So Nellie walked beside the wagon, feeling at peace. Lewis returned from riding to the front of the wagon train, and he offered Blaze for Nellie to ride.

"Thank you, but I am fine," Nellie said. "I don't mind the walk."

She studied the road in front of her. Different-sized rocks jutted out from the dirt. *Just like people,* she thought. All different sizes with different minds and different ways of living their lives. She thought about the Cherokee man who had stolen Midnight to trade for liquor. She whispered a prayer for him and felt better for doing it. She wanted Midnight back, but that was not a bad voice in her mind, that was a fact. Feeling hatred for the man who took the horse was a bad thought.

And what about the white men who took their land? The men who had forced this awful journey on them. *Well, one thing at a time,* she thought. She couldn't silence all the bad voices at once, could she? But she would work on it. With God's help, she would work on accepting change and finding her inner peace. With little steps.

She wanted to tell Morning Sun what she had felt that day, but the road wound up again, and she felt tiredness wash over her as she climbed. Tomorrow, she could run forward and talk with her friend again.

But the next day was a day of snow, light all day long, and Nellie stuck close to the wagon to help with still another sick woman who rode in Old Rivers's wagon.

The following day, she bundled up in four layers of clothes and ran forward to Morning Sun's wagon shortly after the group started down the long trail. But Morning Sun wasn't on the wagon seat.

"Where is she?" Nellie called to Morning Sun's brother, who rode next to his edoda.

"In the back," he said. "She's sick."

CHAPTER 12
Morning Sun

"Sick? With the cold?" Nellie asked Morning Sun's brother.

"Sick with a fever," he said.

"Oh, no. Oh, no!" she wailed. Surely Morning Sun didn't have the bilious fever or whooping cough. "Can I see her?"

Morning Sun's edoda pulled on the reins and paused the horses long enough for Nellie to climb on the back of the wagon.

The inside was dark and as cold as outside. After her eyes adjusted to the dimness, Nellie could see Morning Sun lying on a buildup of wooden boxes that served as a bed. She was shivering, even though she was covered with two blankets. Her etsi squatted on the pile of boxes, her head not two inches from the top of the wagon canvas.

Nellie climbed the boxes and crawled until she could reach Morning Sun's hand. It was burning hot with fever.

At her touch, Morning Sun opened her eyes.

"Nellie?" she said, followed by a racking cough.

"Your cold is worse," Nellie said. "What can I get you? Water?"

Morning Sun's etsi shook her head and pointed at a nearby water bucket.

"I'll get Etsi to fix a poultice. She makes a foul smelling concoction that she puts on a rag around my neck. The bad smell may be what makes the cold go away," Nellie said with a nervous laugh. "It hasn't failed yet."

"I'll be okay," Morning Sun said. The deep cough once again followed her words.

"Don't talk. I'll be back with the poultice."

But it wasn't as simple as Nellie hoped. Etsi said the poultice required brewing, and there wasn't a fire until the wagons stopped in the late afternoon. As soon as the first fire was lit, Nellie put a small amount of water on to boil and stood at the back of the wagon as Etsi rustled through her herb sack for mint leaves. She had already set out some animal fat and her bottle of pine resin to add later.

"Etsi." Sarah was calling from just inside the wagon, where she had ridden all day. Etsi had carved out a little place among the boxes and supplies so she could look out but stay out of the wind's chill. The last couple hours she had been asleep.

"Etsi's busy. What is it?" Nellie walked to the front of the wagon.

"I don't feel good," Sarah said on a whimper.

"Sarah!" Nellie scaled the side. "Where do you hurt?"

"My head and my throat and my all over," Sarah said and coughed.

"Oh, no. Oh, no!" Nellie couldn't stand the thought of both Morning Sun and Sarah sick. "I'm going to make you a bed, Sarah, and I'll stay with you and nurse you. You'll be well in no time."

"In Old Rivers's wagon?" Sarah asked. Her eyes were bright with fever, and when Nellie grabbed her hand, it was as hot as Morning Sun's.

"No, and not in the tent. I'll fix us a special place in this wagon. We'll keep you away from Etsi so she doesn't get sick and make the baby sick. This will be our special place."

Nellie rushed to Etsi and told her to double the potion. Then she climbed in the back of the wagon and moved boxes around until she made a flat space atop the boxes where Sarah could lie down. Her head was near the canvas wagon covering, but that didn't matter.

"I'm so cold," Sarah said.

"We'll fix that," Nellie said. As gently as she could, she wrestled Sarah into several more layers of clothes. Some were Sarah's and some were Nellie's that she dug out of the spots where they had been stuffed. They were unused to cold weather like this, and they had no coats like the white men wore who sold them supplies. Only Lewis's jacket had been packed. They had no extra blankets. The suppliers hadn't brought enough, so Edoda had not gotten any since they had brought some with them. But their blankets were thin, and they were so dirty. They had served as pallets under the wagon, laid on the bare ground. But that couldn't be helped now.

Nellie carried one blanket to the fire and held it close until it was warm. She wrapped Sarah in it and took her own blanket and did the same, switching off the blankets as they grew cold.

"Nellie, will I die?" Sarah asked in a small voice.

"No, honey. You just have a cold, that's all. You've been sick before. Remember that time close to Christmas last year when you were in bed for a week with the croup?"

"Will I be in bed for a week this time?"

"Maybe even less. I'll be right back."

She carried a blanket out to warm.

"Is the poultice ready?" she asked.

"It has not cooked down but soon," Etsi said. "You stir. I'll take the blanket to Sarah."

"No!" Nellie had always obeyed Etsi, but she would not hear of her mother tending to Sarah. She blocked her way when Etsi started toward the wagon. "Etsi, I'll nurse her. She'll be fine. You can talk to her from a distance, but don't go near her. Think about the baby."

"I'm thinking about my daughter," Etsi said.

Edoda had walked up behind them. "Nellie is right," he said. "Lewis and I have the tent up. You need to stay there tonight. Nellie is a brave girl. She can nurse Sarah."

Etsi lowered her head, and Nellie could no longer see her anguished eyes.

"She will be fine. But if there is a change, I'll get you," Nellie promised.

As soon as the poultice was cooked down to a salve consistency and cooled some, Nellie took the warm goop and rubbed it on Sarah's throat and chest. She covered the poultice with one of Lewis's shirts and tied the arms around Sarah's neck to keep it in place.

"Take this to Morning Sun," she told Lewis. "Tell her about Sarah and that I'll check on her as soon as I can."

Lewis rode away on Blaze, and Nellie took up her station in the wagon. She bathed Sarah's face in cold water to lower her fever.

Lewis returned and said Morning Sun was asleep, but her etsi would put the poultice on her.

"Take my coat to Sarah," he told Nellie.

"No, I'm already using your shirts for her. Besides, you need to stay warm, or you'll be sick. But thanks," Nellie said.

Edoda checked on Sarah and reported to Etsi, who stayed away but whose worried voice could be heard right outside the wagon as she brewed up a mixture of butterfly weed with other herbs for Sarah and Morning Sun to swallow to help their coughs. Then she made a healing drink of slippery elm bark. When both were ready, she carried some to the back of the wagon for Nellie and sent Lewis to take some to Morning Sun.

Edoda brought the white doctor, but he was there only a moment and said Nellie was doing the right things. Then he left to go on to the next sick person.

Sarah fell asleep, and an exhausted Nellie lay down beside her. In the night, she warmed the blankets again and covered them both, snuggling close to Sarah to share her body heat.

Nellie awakened before sunrise and built up the campfire so she could heat the blankets. Sarah's forehead was hot to touch, but Nellie believed it was not as hot as it had been the day before. Was she gaining on this awful disease? And what exactly was it that Sarah had? Just a cold, or the more complicated lung disease that kept claiming the lives of the Cherokee on this forced march?

Sarah wouldn't eat any broth and barely choked down the cough medicine before it was time for the wagons to roll. Nellie warmed the blankets once more before the fires were extinguished. She hoped Morning Sun's etsi was doing the same for her.

Nellie lay by Sarah all day, hating the bumpy ride that jarred her until her teeth rattled. She welcomed the rest stops and welcomed Jesse Bushyhead's order for forward riders to build fires along the way so the travelers could warm up. There still wasn't much firewood, and future wagon trains would have to go farther from the road to find dead dry wood, but right now the problem was survival. The walkers suffered mightily from the cold, the poor food, and exhaustion.

Many times Etsi stuck her head in the opening at the front of the wagon, and Nellie would reassure her that Sarah was doing better.

When a halt was called for making camp, Nellie thankfully climbed out of the wagon. She vowed not to complain again about walking, because riding felt even worse.

Etsi brewed another batch of poultice. When Lewis returned from taking the medicine to Morning Sun, Nellie was standing beside the fire, warming a blanket for Sarah. Lewis jumped off Blaze and wouldn't look at Nellie. He ran for Etsi.

"What's wrong?" Nellie called to him, but he wouldn't answer.

Etsi listened to Lewis's low words, bowed her head, and then walked toward Nellie.

"What's wrong?" Nellie asked again. Fear gripped her heart. She couldn't breathe. Tears welled in her eyes, and she knew before Etsi told her.

"Morning Sun has passed on."

"No!" Nellie screamed. "No, that's not true!"

"It is true, Nellie." Etsi grabbed her and pulled her as close as her extended belly would allow. "She is with God now, and she is no longer hurting."

Nellie sobbed. Her shoulders heaved. "Why?" she whispered. "Why?"

"That is not in our power to answer," Etsi said. "It is God's way, and we must accept it."

Nellie sniffed and wiped her face with her hand. "I'm tired of accepting, and I'm tired of forgiving." She took deep ragged breaths. "I'm so tired." She dissolved in another round of sobs that racked her spirit.

"We must see what we can do to help Morning Sun's family with the burial," Etsi said.

Nellie nodded, but she didn't turn loose of Etsi until Sarah called from the wagon for a drink.

"I'll get it," Nellie said as Etsi made a move toward the newly filled water bucket.

Etsi stepped to the wagon and talked to Sarah, but she didn't crawl inside. Instead, she told Nellie she would check on the burial.

With a heavy, heavy heart, Nellie wiped her tears and carried water to Sarah. Her sister was still hot with fever, and a new terror gripped Nellie's soul. What if Sarah was next to go?

Her tears flowed anew, and Sarah asked what was wrong.

"Morning Sun died."

"Was she the same sick as me?"

"No. She was much worse. You are going to get well," Nellie vowed and shook her fist at death. She would battle until her own dying breath before she let death take her sister.

"Here, Sarah, I'm going to put a new poultice on your chest. This is going to help you get better fast."

She smeared on the salve, covered it, and wrapped Sarah in a warmed blanket.

"You must drink the broth tonight. You hear me?" Nellie gripped Sarah's shoulders harder than she meant to. "You have to eat to get your strength back. You must help, Sarah."

"I think I can swallow it, but Nellie, I couldn't do it yesterday." Tears flowed down Sarah's cheeks. "I don't want to be sick. I want to help."

"I know. I know. I'm sorry if I sound upset with you. I'm not.

It's not your fault you're sick. I'll get you some broth."

The supper was merely salt pork broth, and Sarah drank as much as she could, and then she said she would try to drink some more. "This will help me," Sarah said.

"Yes, it will. That's a good girl, Sarah."

Nellie waited until Sarah was asleep, and then she slipped out of the wagon.

"Nellie." Old Rivers beckoned her to the fireside. "I am sorry about your friend. It is hard."

"It is very hard," Nellie said.

"Your parents are with her family. They will bury her tomorrow morning before we leave."

Nellie never saw Morning Sun again. Her body was wrapped in one of the precious blankets, and she was encased in a coffin of saplings loosely tied together with woody leafless grapevines.

As Reverend Bushyhead prayed over Morning Sun, snow fell softly, sifting through the gaps of the coffin and landing on the blanket.

"She will be cold," Nellie whispered to no one. "She needs a warmed blanket." She bent her head, covered her face with her hands, and moaned. Morning Sun, the bright girl who had a sunny smile and a friendly word for everyone, was gone.

Soon dirt formed a mound over the coffin.

"Let's go, Nellie," Etsi said and put her arms around Nellie's shoulders. They walked back to their wagon and prepared to leave.

Nellie warmed another blanket in front of the fire and pushed it in front of her as she crawled into the wagon to Sarah. She watched out the front slit of the canvas for Morning Sun's grave.

As the wagon passed it, she crawled to the back of the wagon and looked out the back flap at the snow-covered mound.

"Sleep with the angels, my good friend," Nellie whispered. Then she crawled back to squat beside Sarah's bed.

For three more days, the gray sky spit snow, sometimes hard, sometimes softly. And then the sun came out just as the wagons lined up to cross the Ohio River.

Sarah's fever had broken, and she sat inside the wagon with her head barely peeking out of the front slit so she could see the outside world again. Now that Nellie was no longer needed as a nurse, she gratefully accepted a perch on the wagon bench beside Old Rivers.

"Long ago, this was the northern border of Cherokee land," Old Rivers said, as they waited their turn to cross on the ferry.

"We are not halfway there yet, are we?" Nellie asked.

"I heard talk that after we cross the Mississippi, we will be halfway."

"But look how much time has passed already. Etsi's time will come soon. I thought we would be living in the new land before the baby was born." She wondered at the words she was sharing with Old Rivers. In the old times, before this horrible journey, she would not have talked about an indelicate subject like childbirth with an old man. But they had been through rain and snow, death and more death, and hungry times. Not talking about something as important a part of nature as the birth of a baby seemed silly.

"She will be fine no matter where the baby is born," Old Rivers said.

"I pray that is so," Nellie said.

She rode onto the ferry atop his wagon and remembered how she had been astride Midnight when they had taken a ferry across the Tennessee River. John had not crossed that river. Now Morning Sun had not crossed the Ohio. Who would be missing when they arrived at the Mississippi?

CHAPTER 13

The Long Wait

The days of November passed as the Bushyhead wagon train slowly progressed across Illinois. Nellie made it through each day, thanking God for Sarah's recovery but unable to mention Morning Sun and her aching heart in her prayers.

Nellie saw her long face mirrored in the faces of her etsi and the other women. Joy was missing from all eyes. Misery had taken its place.

At Jonesboro, the mill ran extra hours and made planks that were distributed to the Cherokee to use as flooring in their tents. Each evening, Lewis carefully put the planks down to keep out the cold from the ground, and each morning, he was in charge of getting them slipped back into the wagon.

Some of the Cherokee families used their planks to make coffins, as more people died and were buried in unmarked graves beside the road. There were three burials on one day. Nellie did not attend the services. She couldn't. It was too soon after Morning Sun's death to see more coffins lowered into shallow graves.

They traveled on until they were near the banks of the mighty Mississippi River.

They had been delayed at the Tennessee crossing by a wagon train in front of them, but it was nothing compared to the tents and wagons camped beside the ferry road.

"We've caught up with Reverend Jones's group," Edoda told

the family at supper. "They've been waiting some time to cross, but it could be a long wait."

The next day, Lewis and Nellie rode together on Blaze to look at the big river. Ice extended far out from both banks, but in the center of the Mississippi, huge chunks of ice, some the size of cabins, tumbled in the current. The chunks crashed into each other, making a horrific sound. And they kept coming. Night and day, the jagged blocks of ice collided with huge shocks. The sound haunted Nellie's dreams.

The river was not frozen enough for the wagons to drive across, and it was too jammed with ice floes to allow the ferry to cross. They were stuck.

One December week turned into the next, and the camp grew. Another wagon train caught up to them, and there were more slit trenches dug, more funerals held, and the need for more food for people and animals alike.

Yet another wagon train caught up to them, and then another. Food was so scarce some draft mules were killed and butchered for meat. One night, a hard snow blew in that continued the next morning.

Nellie shivered in the tent, huddled with Etsi and Sarah. Edoda and Lewis had gone out in the deep snow for food, but they been gone for some time, and she was beginning to wonder why they had not returned. Old Rivers and Smoke Cloud had gone with them.

Etsi moaned, and Nellie looked at her searchingly. Etsi was strong, and even at their darkest moments, she had kept a countenance of determined, if sometimes forced, cheerfulness. This morning had been different with Etsi's lips drawn in a straight line. Once Nellie caught her biting her lip.

Etsi moaned again, and this time she reached for Nellie's hand and squeezed it so hard Nellie feared her bones were broken.

"Oh, no. It's time!" Nellie grabbed Etsi's other hand. "What can I do?"

"Get Red Blossom. She will help me."

"Sarah, stay with Etsi. Hold her hand. No, give her this flute to bite." The wooden flute had recently been carved by Old Rivers, and Lewis had been trying to play it. It would help Etsi bear the pain.

Nellie rearranged the bed and had Etsi lie down. She took one blanket and wrapped it around her shoulders against the wet snow and stepped out into what had turned into a blizzard.

A couple hours ago when Edoda and Lewis had left, the air was full of flakes. Now it was a complete whiteout, and the snow came halfway to her knees. She could not see two feet ahead of her, so she walked with her arms outstretched, feeling her way toward the wagon of Red Blossom.

"Edoda!" she called out. "Old Rivers!" she shouted in the direction of his wagon, which was on one side of their tent, on the chance the men had returned. The wind whipped her words back at her.

She turned toward the Starr wagon on the other side of their tent. She struggled alongside the wagon and had taken five steps away from it when she looked back over her shoulder and could no longer see it. Panic hit her that she might not find Red Blossom's wagon, which was a distance of some seven wagons. And at her slow pace in the deep snow, she might not make it back in time. She stepped backward, not turning, not taking the chance of getting confused on which direction was the tent. She slipped her feet into the footprints she had left, which were quickly filling with the blowing snow.

Backward step by backward step, she felt her way until she touched the wagon. Was there anything inside that she could use to help deliver the baby? She searched her mind for what Etsi had needed when the last baby had been born, the one that had died.

She gasped. What if this baby died, too? What if she couldn't help Etsi?

"Stop and think," she said out loud, reassured to hear her own voice, which didn't sound as panicked as she felt. There had been hot water, and she remembered talk of a tied cord. She'd need twine and a fire. Something to wrap the baby in. They were wearing everything they could, but surely there was a scrap of material tucked somewhere. She needed firewood, but there was none. The wooden boxes, of course. But how could she tear them apart? The ax that Lewis had rescued from home was near the back, in easy reach when the men needed it.

Her cold fingers struggled to untie the back flap of the wagon, and she climbed inside. Discarding the blanket, she made sure she tucked it right at the end of the wagon, so she could put it back on when she left. The ax was right where it was supposed to be. Her freezing fingers closed around the handle, and she pounded on a box, breaking the small planks into splinters. Good. That would make the flame catch. This box was filled with their good dishes, and she gathered some of the old newspapers Etsi had wrapped them in to use for starting the fire.

She felt between the boxes, shifted boxes and pinched her fingers, but barely felt the pain. She grabbed something soft. In the dim light she saw it was the gingham dress she had worn on the day they had been driven from their home.

Now twine. Oh, the ties for the back flap. She reached into the flying snow and brought the flap inside. With the ax, she awkwardly sawed at the tie until she cut off an end, but had left enough to retie the flap.

She needed the flint rock. Where was it? *Think,* she told herself. *Think.* It should be at the back of the wagon, too, and it was. She wrapped her twine, the splintered wood, the ax, the dress, and the flint rock in the blanket and climbed out, tying the flap as best she could.

She felt along the wagon until she reached the end, and then she asked God to guide the few steps it would take to reach the tent. She groped for it, and sighed when her wet, freezing fingers groped waist-high snow. It was the snow-covered tent!

"Thank You, God," she whispered and felt along for the opening. "I'm back," she said as she stumbled inside. She shook off snow and closed the flap behind her.

"Red Blossom," Etsi said in a weak voice.

"Etsi's real sick," Sarah said. "Real sick."

"The baby's coming," Nellie said. "And you and I are going to help it come."

Sarah's mouth flew open, and her eyes widened. "How?"

"I don't know. Etsi, you will have to tell us what to do. I brought twine and wood for a fire."

"No place. . .for a fire," Etsi said. "No smoke hole." She panted in pain, and Sarah placed the flute in her mouth, obviously a sign they had settled on while Nellie was in the blizzard.

Etsi moaned even while biting on the flute. "It is coming fast," she said when she spit out the flute. A moment later, she was panting again, and Sarah held the flute for her to bite.

"It's coming," Etsi said a moment later. Sweat ran down her face.

"What do I do?" Nellie asked.

"Help me up."

"Up?"

"I need to squat and push," Etsi said between gritted teeth.

"Sarah, grab this arm," Nellie said. "Now." Between the two of them, they got Etsi into a squatting position. "Sarah, stay behind her; let her lean on you."

"Feel. . .the. . .baby," Etsi gasped.

Nellie knelt in front of Etsi and instinctively reached under her.

"I can feel its head. Push, Etsi, push."

Etsi took a deep breath and pushed. In a *whoosh*, Nellie felt a sticky weight in her hands. She looked in wonder at the bloody baby as Etsi collapsed back on Sarah.

"Lay her down," she yelled at Sarah, who was desperately trying to keep Etsi upright.

Nellie used a corner of a blanket to dry off the now-screaming baby.

"Here, Etsi. Praise God. He is alive," Nellie said. She laid the little boy on Etsi's still swollen belly.

"The afterbirth is coming," Etsi said. "And you will need to cut the cord."

Their sharp knife was with Edoda. With no other way, Nellie took the ax, placed the baby and the long cord that connected the baby to the afterbirth on the floor, and with one hard swing, cut the cord. She wiped the baby's end of the cord with the blanket, wrapped the baby in her gingham dress, and handed him to Etsi.

"I'll be right back," she said. She slipped outside, carrying the afterbirth. She cleared the snow in front of the flap with the ax, chopped a hole in the frozen earth, and buried the afterbirth. She washed her bloody hands in the snow, shook snow off her head and shoulders, and went back inside.

Etsi was smiling. "The baby is perfect," she said. "Girls, you did a wonderful job. Thank you."

"Can you feed the baby?" Nellie asked.

"I will try. Do we have any water?"

Nellie broke the ice on the top of the water bucket and filled the dipper. Etsi drank.

"It is so cold," she said and shivered.

"We need a fire," Nellie said.

She rearranged the bed for Etsi, and covered her and the baby with all the blankets in the room except the one Sarah was bundled in.

The baby needed warmth. A flame, even a tiny flame would help. Too bad they had long ago used up the kerosene in their lamps.

"Etsi," she cried. "Did you pack any candles? Any at all?" In the back of her mind she remembered Etsi packing the candle molds.

"I'm unsure," Etsi said. "We have used none."

There were some. Nellie knew it. They'd been in the kitchen when Etsi had mentioned them. She would go look.

"Watch them," Nellie told Sarah. "I'll be back." The snow was not so thick this time, but Nellie still took every precaution against losing her way. In the back of the wagon, she dug through the box of good dishes and found the candles. Six of them. Not many, but it was a start.

When she finally made it back to the tent, she lit a candle by sparking the flint rock next to an issue of the *Cherokee Phoenix*. Too bad about the treasured papers, but they were nothing when measured next to her little brother's life.

With the paper afire, she lit the candle, and then stomped out the paper fire, saving what she could. She took off a shirt and held it next to the flame. It wasn't much, but the fabric was warmed. She unwrapped the baby and wrapped him in the warmed shirt, and she held the gingham dress to the flame.

Stomping outside warned her an instant before Edoda and Lewis came inside the tent, carrying a sack of provisions and letting in the wind-driven snow.

"What is this?" Edoda said.

"You have another son," Nellie announced proudly.

Edoda and Lewis made their way over to Etsi and the baby.

"We must find a way to build a fire to keep him warm," Nellie said, "or he will. . ." She couldn't complete her thought. But in her mind she knew the baby could die. "We will be out of candles soon."

"The main cooking fires have blown out from the storm, so building a fire will probably not work. But we can warm the baby ourselves." Edoda took off his layered shirts, held the baby next to his warm skin, and put the shirts back on. "Lewis, get Old Rivers and Smoke Cloud. And be careful."

While Lewis was gone, Edoda explained how the whiteout kept them trapped at the supply wagon. "The snow has let up some," he said.

"I know," Nellie said and explained about her trips to the wagon.

Old Rivers and Smoke Cloud came into the tent. The heat from the candle and the body heat from so many in the tent raised the temperature a bit. They took turns holding the baby inside their shirts. Then they gave him back to Etsi to nurse.

By the end of the day, the storm had blown through. The temperature was frigid, but the men made a short lean-to from the canvas flap on the wagon and built a fire to keep blankets warmed. They chopped up more boxes for firewood.

"Nellie," Old Rivers said, "you have done much today. You are brave."

Nellie, tired to her bones, smiled.

CHAPTER 14

The New Land

The Bushyhead group spent nearly a month beside the Mississippi River before the members were ferried across at Moccasin Springs. It was a month of hunger and cold, but Nellie and the others were busy keeping little Snow Bird alive. He was given a Cherokee name because it had not helped them to name the other children with English names, Etsi said.

"I would like a Cherokee name," Nellie said.

"You have one," Old Rivers said. "She-Who-Is-Brave. Nellie the Brave."

"That is exactly the one for you," Etsi said. "You have earned it."

Many Cherokee died in the camp. Jesse Bushyhead's sister was buried by the river. He named his own baby daughter, born just after the crossing into Missouri, Eliza Missouri Bushyhead.

"Snow Bird and Eliza will be in the same class in school," Nellie said when they heard of the birth.

"Yes," said Edoda. "Now we have to get to the new land and build that school."

The trip across Missouri was not as long as the first part of the journey. Even though the bitter winter took its toll on all of them, Nellie took joy from holding Snow Bird's little fingers and listening to his coos and watching for his smiles.

The roads varied from bumpy to muddy to deeply rutted to no road at all. Day after day after day, Nellie walked, fixed meager meals from sometimes wormy cornmeal, fell asleep in the tent that now had rips in it, and always was cold and hungry and tired, so tired.

What got her through each day was the number of miles they made, sometimes just five, sometimes ten, each taking them closer to the land where they could build a new house and she could go to school again.

She longed for a bath. She washed her hands and face daily, but her clothes and the rest of her hadn't seen hot water and soap in months. She was actually daydreaming about soaking in a washtub with hot water steaming around her when she heard a shout from Old Rivers in the wagon behind her.

It all happened in slow motion. One moment she was walking beside the wagon, and the next the right wheel of the wagon was coming straight at her. She had no time to dodge it, but she put her hands up to deflect the blow from her face, although it knocked her to the ground. At the same time, she saw the wagon tip dangerously to the side, and she thought it was going to turn over and kill her parents and her sister and new brother. Edoda's quick actions, turning the oxen in the opposite direction, kept the wagon upright.

Etsi screamed, Sarah in her little spot inside the wagon screamed, Snow Bird wailed. But no one was really hurt. Except Nellie. She lay on the road with the heavy wheel on top of her foot, which was twisted at an odd angle.

Old Rivers got to her first and lifted the wheel. He immediately took off her high moccasin, revealing an ankle that was already starting to swell. He carried her to his wagon and somehow managed to place her on the driver's seat. She knew she was no help at all in climbing into the wagon.

Behind them, the wagons stopped, but walkers went around on the side of the road. Smoke Cloud helped Etsi and the others out of the Starr wagon on the side with two wheels. Etsi hurried to Nellie.

"Where are you hurt?"

"My ankle." It really didn't hurt, but the growing size of her ankle told her it was badly injured. Blood trickled from scratches on her forearms.

"The baby?"

"He is fine. We are not hurt, but we must take care of you. Put your foot up on the seat. We will have the doctor look at it."

That the white doctor was being summoned meant it could be something really bad. He was not much good at stopping the illnesses that raced through the Cherokee, but he was knowledgeable about broken bones. Surely she had not broken her foot. It was starting to ache now, but that was all.

Lewis had been riding farther back in the line with a friend, but he now rode up to see what the delay was. Etsi sent him for the doctor.

Smoke Cloud and Edoda righted the wheel and rolled it to the axle. They used a wagon jack to raise the wagon until they could slip the wheel back on, and then they repaired the hub to keep the wheel attached.

"I don't know how that came off," Edoda said. "It's fortunate the wheel wasn't broken."

The doctor rode back with Lewis, and he examined Nellie's foot.

"Sprained," he said. "Not broken. Don't walk on it for a while."

"How long?" Nellie asked. Even in her pain, she was glad to practice her English with the doctor. It had been a long time since she had spoken her second language.

"A week, ten days," he said.

Nellie passed the long hours riding on the driver's seat next to Old Rivers. For a Cherokee who believed silence was golden and that words gained much power once they were spoken aloud, he turned into a regular chatterbox beside her.

He had found eagle feathers during the month they had been camped beside the Mississippi and before the great blizzard came. He was going to give them to Lewis when they reached the new land.

He talked to Nellie about the balance she needed in her life.

"Right now, the physical has taken over because your foot needs care," he said, "but you must also think of your mind and your spirit."

"I think of those things," Nellie said. One evening she showed him the journal that she had kept sporadically. Too many times she was too tired at night to write in the journal, and riding in the wagon and writing was impossible.

"What did you write about Morning Sun?" Old Rivers asked.

"I wrote about our time in the camp all summer and about us walking together on this horrible trail. That is all."

"You did not write about her death?"

"I could not."

"Nellie, you must not hold the bitterness inside."

"I am not bitter."

"Remember our talk about the bad voices, the bad thoughts of hate in our minds that rob us of inner peace?"

"I remember. And I remember you said that it takes little steps to still the voices."

"But are you trying to still the thoughts at all? Or are you letting hatred build inside? In your mind and heart?"

Nellie was silent for a long time. She lowered her head and sighed a sigh that came from deep inside her heart. Nothing would bring back Morning Sun.

"The white men killed Morning Sun by forcing us on this horrible trip."

"That may be true or may not be true. She may have caught the disease in the old land."

Again Nellie was silent for a long moment. "Maybe."

The next day on the wagon, Old Rivers brought it up again. Nellie didn't want to talk about it, but he would not let her be silent.

"Yes, you are right that she might have died anyway."

"Death is the end of living as we know it. That is all. We should celebrate Morning Sun's life here with us, and we should celebrate that she was a Christian who has gone to her reward. We should remember her with pleasure, which honors her, not think of her and let hate for others take over."

"Don't you believe the Cherokee way is not to talk? Not to give power to words?"

"That is true, but the words come when the right person is here to share the words."

"And you are that right person?"

"No. You are that right person for me," Old Rivers said. "I must also still the bad thoughts. It helps me to talk to you about your feelings because they are much like my own."

Nellie's eyes widened. No matter if a person were old or young, they shared the same feelings. And they had to overcome the same bad feelings.

"Not having forgiveness in your heart hurts you. It causes real damage. Not forgiving someone is like building a stone wall around your heart and mind so you cannot move forward."

"How do you forgive?"

"I pray to the one true God for the strength to silence the bad thoughts and to let me forgive those who have harmed me."

"I will do that, too," Nellie said. She bowed her head and prayed for strength to still the bad thoughts, the strength to forgive the white men, and the ability to find inner peace.

She smiled at Old Rivers. He smiled back. It was the first honest-to-goodness smile she had seen on his lined face—ever.

"Remember, the thoughts sometimes come back, so we must pray daily for the strength."

"I will," she said. She had listened to Reverend Bushyhead's services, and she had recited some prayers by rote, but this one had come from her heart. It gave her new peace.

"You must write about Morning Sun in your journal," Old Rivers said.

That night, Nellie wrote a long letter to Morning Sun, telling her how empty and angry and bitter she'd felt when Morning Sun had died. It made her feel better to share her inner thoughts with her friend, even though her friend would never read the words.

After a week on Old Rivers's wagon seat, Nellie began walking a little bit each day. Three weeks later, she was walking like normal again. She was walking when the group crossed into Arkansas.

"It won't be long now," Edoda said. "Maybe a couple more weeks."

Cherokee spirits seemed to lift at the thought of journey's end. They traveled longer each day, covering more miles but fighting the gray skies of winter. The temperature was warmer than when they had camped that miserable month near the Mississippi. And the snows did not last as long before the sun melted them.

Even so, some Cherokee did not finish this part of the long journey but were buried alongside the road. Those times were hard for Nellie, and she prayed especially hard for strength to fight bitterness.

The day came when Lewis galloped from near the front of the long train.

"We have crossed into the new territory," he said.

"Are we there?" Nellie asked.

"Not exactly where we are headed, but we're in the new land," he said.

Nellie looked at the landscape with new interest. The road was barely a path, and it still had deep ruts where the wagons traveled but with the gray grass of winter in between. The hills gently rolled. Some were wooded, and others were already cleared for fields. Pines and cedars were the only green trees, but they were enough to set off the gray and brown winter skeletons of the ash, oak, hickory, and elms. Wild grapevines curled among the limbs.

Nellie hitched a ride with Old Rivers when they came to a creek. Crystal clear water gurgled around the stones. Along the bank, willow trees leaned toward the water.

They camped for the night and rode farther into the new territory the next day. On February 27, they made their last camp as a group. They had arrived. Nellie could hardly believe she had thought they would make the journey in less than three months.

It had taken double that time, and the suffering along the trail had been great.

Reverend Bushyhead held a prayerful service. He announced that by his calculations, they had lost 38 of their number to death. Nellie thought of She-Who-Sings and Morning Sun. Reverend Bushyhead said on the happy side, there had been six births on the journey. Snow Bird was among that happy number. And out of the original 950 Cherokee to begin the journey, 148 had deserted. Nellie counted John and the Deerborn family among that number, and she added a special prayer for their safety and happiness.

Where to build a house? Who was in charge? There were so many things to consider, but Edoda said they would build a log cabin not too far from the Cherokee Baptist Mission where Reverend Bushyhead's family was going to live. When the settlement money from Edoda's old store came in from the white government, he hoped to start another store. He picked a building site for their cabin not far from a creek, and wasting not a moment, he, Smoke Cloud, Lewis, and Old Rivers began sawing down trees.

March blew in, and with it, signs of spring were everywhere. Spring was in the warm breeze that came from the south on days when the sky was the blue of a new robin's egg. Green buds appeared on trees, and wild crocus bloomed yellow and pink.

By summer, the Starr family lived in a small cabin, Old Rivers and Smoke Cloud with them. It was not at all like the nice house they had had in Tennessee, but it was a new home. On a shelf, Nellie placed the glass bottle with the silver inlay she had rescued from their old front parlor. Next to it ticked the mantle clock from the old house. They used the good dishes for meals, which reminded her of the old life.

Beside the house, Nellie had made a little flower garden. Mixed among the stones and rocks that formed the border, she had placed the five stones she had brought from Tennessee. They were a reminder of the past, but they were mixed with new stones to show that she was a combination of her past and her present.

Now Nellie sat on the front porch in a new rocking chair that Old Rivers had made. She held Snow Bird, who reached up his little hand and played with Nellie's gold cross necklace. Old Rivers had given it to her and said that treasures were people, not things, and that he wanted her to wear the cross.

He had taught her to pray to stop the bad thoughts of fear and hatred, and they had gone. A song burst from her heart for a new beginning, and she sang a lullaby to her little brother.

ANOTHER NOTE TO READERS

The Cherokee who completed the journey over the Trail of Tears were not finished with hard times. Those who had signed the false treaty that forced the 1838 removal of the Cherokee were assassinated. The old Cherokee settlers, who had been many years in Indian Territory, and the new Cherokee immigrants fought to head the government. A time of lawlessness reigned for several years.

Finally, the Cherokee settled down under one government and organized public schools, courts, and a Cherokee–English newspaper.

The fight with the white government was not over. Later legislation took tribal ownership from the Cherokee and gave acreage to individual Indians. The rest was sold to white men with the fees given to the Cherokee government.

In 1907, the state of Oklahoma was established from Indian Territory. Although today's Cherokee are citizens of the United States, they maintain their own Cherokee Nation headquarters in Tahlequah, Oklahoma, and elect their own councils. Many students study their oral language and Sequoyah's syllabary. The *Cherokee Phoenix,* a newspaper printed with articles in English and in Cherokee, is still being published today.

If you enjoyed

Nellie
the Brave

be sure to read other

SISTERS IN TIME

books from BARBOUR PUBLISHING

American colon... *Dust Bowl* *World war* *Civil war* *Frontier*

- Perfect for Girls Ages Eight to Twelve

- History and Faith in Intriguing Stories

- Lead Character Overcomes Personal Challenge

- Covers Seventeenth to Twentieth Centuries

- Collectible Series of 24 Titles

6" x 8¼" / Paperback / 144 pages / $4.97

AVAILABLE WHEREVER CHRISTIAN BOOKS ARE SOLD